## CHAPTER ONE

"Hey, I've just had a really great idea!" Ellie pushed a stray lock of hair behind her ears as she spoke, eyes wide open with enthusiasm. "Why don't you adopt me?" She sat on the bed cross legged, school tie loose, auburn hair bursting out of its clips, uniform trashed.

I looked up at her, smiling, expecting to see a mischievous smile in return. But there was none. Ellie looked as if she was about to burst with excitement as she looked straight at me, obviously waiting for my answer.

I didn't answer. I was too shocked. I felt the colour drain out of my face and my heart skipped a beat. She carried on undaunted.

"Remember you said adoption's best for me? You're my social worker. You've done a great job. We get on great. I think you and Dr Angus should be my parents now." She underlined her statement by pointing in my direction.

I expected that final twist even less. "You are joking?" I replied, "Why Dr Angus?" I pulled a face in surprise. Who would want to marry me anyway? Certainly not anyone as nice as him, I thought to myself. Surely he couldn't want to marry a social worker who can't even fix her own problems? If anyone had asked me two minutes ago what the craziest thing ever to happen to me could be, this would be it, top of the list, number one slot.

I gathered my senses and remembered I was a professional and Ellie had been through a lot. I admired her pluck and courage in not having given up on the world and I could understand her need to find stability after what she had been through. I suppose it was good that she still had confidence in the idea of family and wanted to be part of one. I wondered how to let her down gently.

“I can barely look after myself never mind anyone else!” I furrowed my brow, half- smiling, half serious and replied. “What's Gus done to deserve me? I’d be a hopeless mum. I burn supper. I’m always late home from work. Dinner is sometimes just a tin of beans and an apple. I’m never at home long enough to be a wife and mum,” I laughed, hoping that making a joke out of such a strange suggestion would make it go away.

It didn’t.

“You don’t have to be like that, you could change you know.” Ellie continued, her gaze taking on a steely determination. “You said last week families aren’t just about food and cooking, it’s about love and care. And Dr Gus really fancies you. His eyes go all loved up when you’re around. Even I can see that." She sounded almost like a counsellor herself now, a tone I suspect she’d learnt from her Nan.

Why is it twelve- year- olds always think they know everything? To say I was speechless was the understatement of the year. I scanned Ellie’s face for signs of laughter again, but still there was nothing. Surely she couldn’t be serious? Did she really mean me? Perhaps she meant someone else. I looked at her and my heart melted. I was totally taken aback at her directness that's for sure, but it was also that spark of life that made her just so loveable, the guts she had for whatever life threw at her to just get up and get on with it again. But there wasn't an easy way out of this situation, for me being with someone would mean facing risk. And I wasn't about to do that.

I thought long and hard. I let myself imagine the scenario thinking some obvious problem would pop out at me and I could explain it to Ellie and that would be the end of it. So I thought of Angus, Ellie & I out for a picnic on the beach, or shopping in the local town, or round the tree at Christmas, or going to school events. But far from being unpleasant I was quite surprised. It didn't seem so bad after all.

A shiver ran down my spine, one that I was faintly starting to recognise, every time Dr Angus was around. So far I'd been quite good at ignoring it, or so I told myself. I took a deep breath and looked out of the window, desperately trying to find an answer for Ellie, but how do you sum up a major relationship phobia in one easy sentence?

But then it occurred to me. Part of what I love about Ellie is her guts, her sheer bravery in the face of life. And I admired that. I suddenly I thought, if she can do it, shouldn't I be able, as the adult professional, to be able to do the same thing?

Anyway, to start the story here is not to tell you the beginning, which explains how I got here in the first place or why I had such a turmoil in my mind. I was out to change my life when I moved here, that's for sure, but just how much was something I would never have dreamed of.

I was escaping Edinburgh and the personal troubles I'd had when I first reached Drummond Moor Island that chilly April morning, before I'd met Ellie or Dr Angus or any of the people who would later play such an important part in my life. On my first day the boat chugged into the harbour and I watched as it pulled into its mooring place. The cool morning air chilled my cheeks and the salty tang of the sea was like a tonic. For the first time in years I felt fresh and alive. This was the new start I wanted, the chance to brush away the cobwebs of my old life and start again. It had been a long time coming and many times I'd questioned whether I was doing the right thing by leaving my flat and all the people I knew at such a difficult time, even for just six months. But now I was actually really here any doubts I'd had melted away. If there was any part of the world beautiful enough to nurse me back to life again, this was it.

My car bumped over the boards driving from boat to land, I checked the map and road signs to my new place of work. The letter offering me the post said. 'You'll be based at St Columba's Surgery, Old Court. Start on Monday the first, 10am.' That was where I was interviewed for the six month post. I remembered it with pleasure and followed the coast road to my future.

It seemed to take forever to get there but that was probably just my impatience. Eventually I arrived and as I pulled into the car park I noticed a tall, professional- looking man, doctor's bag in his right hand, left hand resting casually in his trousers pocket, waiting at the surgery entrance. A thatch of nut brown hair almost covered his eyes, and he leaned against the wall, buffeting himself against the wind. He looked kind, honest, gentle, as far as you can tell just by looks. His clothes, rather than the city fashions I was used to, looked lived in, well-worn without being shabby. They were natural fabrics, Harris Tweed, wool, cotton, linen, and they draped around him like old friends. I guess it was because of his homely appearance which gave him he had a look of honesty and sincerity about him and I had to remind myself not to judge people by their looks.

I followed another car in, and two more cars drove in behind me. At first, he seemed to be scanning the occupants of each vehicle, but soon his gaze rested on me and I could see it was me he was interested in. He watched as I pulled into a parking space and walked towards me. He looked a little stressed, not out of control, but as if he was worried about something. I rolled down the window as he got nearer.

"Excuse me," he began. "Would you be the new social worker by any chance?" he asked. He had a beautiful local accent and rolled his 'R's with a musical chime.

"I am." I replied simply, wondering why he wanted to know.

"Good." I saw him breathe a sigh of relief, "I've been waiting for you. I'm Gus, Dr Angus McGlone, Duty Mental Health GP here today." He thrust his arm through my open window to shake hands.

"Louise Kimber, Social Worker." I shook his hand. "Nice to meet you."

"Listen, I'm sorry about the unusual welcome," he said explained, "but the managers didnae feel they had any choice. We've been asked to go out on an emergency. It's a young girl, 13 years old, who is really stressed at school and the staff think she might be suicidal. The teachers have left her in a room by herself and don't know what to do with her. She hasn't been seen by a social worker before and there' is nothing except childhood illnesses on her medical records, so no relevant previous history at all. That's my blue car over there," he pointed to it. "If you follow me we can go there straight away. I've got to go on and do my rounds afterwards, so we need separate cars."

Concern welled up inside me. It's awful to think of but the teenage suicide rate is pretty high and I could see why this situation needed immediate attention. "I guess it's a Mental Health Act Assessment, she might need to be admitted to a psychiatric hospital." I said, half thinking out loud.

Gus nodded in agreement, his hair blowing in the breeze as he spoke. "Aye, she might indeed." He replied and briskly walked off to his car.

It wasn't quite the welcome I had been expecting. The usual thing when you start a new job is to meet your colleagues, have a cup of tea, find your desk and learn how to use the computer system. But by law you need a specially qualified doctor and social worker in mental health emergencies like this, because we could admit a person to hospital even if they objected, if we thought they were too ill to make a rational decision and needed inpatient hospital care. If the team I was about to join were short- staffed, I guess there wasn't time to start with the niceties and they had no choice other than to send us out even if it was my first day. After all, mental health was my specialism and the lack of specialist staff meant I'd was often being called out on emergencies at any time of the day or night.

I worried about the young girl we were about to see. I'm always concerned about the people I visit, but such a young girl feeling low enough to think of suicide made me doubly sad. Taking away someone's liberty and giving them the stigma of having been sectioned is a very serious step and not one ever undertaken lightly, especially when the subject is so young. But there were times when it was necessary to save a life.

And this could be one of those times.

I followed the doctor's car along the rocky headland for a couple of miles until we reached another part of town. Soon we arrived at a big modern school with students milling about everywhere, heads down, shoulders hunched against the biting wind.

We pulled up side by side outside the school. I looked at Dr McGlone, Gus as he called himself, more closely. Despite the urgency he looked calm and approachable, yet somehow he exuded an air of competence but not bossiness. Just right for a GP, I thought.

He waited for me to finish locking my car and we walked in together. "It seems a wee bit of a shame having to drag you out like this in your new job before you've even stepped in the door," he sympathised. "But the social work department, who you probably remember, are in the same building as us, told me it couldn't be helped."

"Don't worry about it." I smiled matching his pace, "These things happen. I'm used to it." And I was. Every social work office I'd ever been in was always frantically busy. Mostly it felt just like being in a busy market places, with people hurrying about, busily working on phones and computers. It was no surprise to me that even social work offices on remote islands ones were just as busy.

Gus opened the door for me and we introduced ourselves at reception.

Moments later a smart, efficient- looking woman in a tweed suit bustled along the corridor to meet us. She carried a clipboard, held her head high, and had an air of tolerating no nonsense about her.

"I'm so pleased to see ye both." She shook our hands firmly. "I'm Mrs McComber. Shirley McComber. Head of English at St Columba's. If you follow me I'll take you in." She looked tense despite her smile, and we hurried up the corridor behind her.

She paused to let some pupils past and I took the opportunity to speak to her. "Could you tell us a little about the problem, and give us a bit of background on the girl before we meet her, please?"  It's not as easy to understand someone's behaviour if you haven't got background knowledge of them and getting a full a history of their lives really helps when you meet them for the first time.

"Of course. Follow me." Shirley replied crisply. "We'll go somewhere we can't be overheard."

I wondered if the teachers were a bit irritated with Ellie. It could be very humiliating for them to have a pupil so out of control they had to call in outside help and Shirley didn't seem to me to be the compassionate type. Angus and I followed her down a dark corridor until we came to a little gathering of people outside a room. Shirley took us to a quiet corner.

"Ellie Grant, the girl we're worried about, is in there," Shirley whispered, nodding in the direction of a classroom. "We've had to move the pupils that should be in there to another room. Ellie just wouldn't leave. She's pacing up and down crying and crying yet not speaking to anyone. We've all tried talking to her, but she didn't answer and worse still doesn't even seem to notice we're there." She indicated the group of people. "I'm worried she'll attempt suicide, she can't seem to control herself."

"Has she mentioned suicide?" Angus asked with authority.

It would be helpful to know if Ellie had mentioned it, or if it was just a teacher's fears?

"Yes. One of the other girls said she had spoken to her about it, and knowing the other girl I'm inclined to believe her. When you see how distressed she is you'll see what we mean. We've found it impossible to get through to her. She lives with her Nan, who I'm told is ill at the moment. One of our staff knows her neighbour who vaguely knows the family, so it's not a completely reliable source, but she believes its cancer." Shirley explained, looking from one to the other of us, "Apparently Ellie is staying with a neighbour at the moment. We've been trying to ring the neighbour on the number we've been given to get her to come and take Ellie home, she's obviously not well enough for school. But we can't get through."

"Poor Ellie. It sounds like she might already have had a lot of trauma in her life, if she's no parents to live with," I sympathised. "We need to know whether she's safe at the neighbours though and they'll need to be assessed to check that. Does Ellie have a history of mental health problems at school? Does she often do things like this?"

"She's had her bad days that's for sure," Shirley puffed up her chest and replied curtly. "A few detentions for not doing her homework, talking in class, that sort of thing. Nothing like this though."

"Who are all the people outside?" Angus asked, looking in their direction.

Shirley turned to face them and indicated them discreetly as she spoke. "Three are teachers, two are police women. I called the police when she wouldn't listen to us. We've all tried speaking to her but got nowhere. She shouted to us to get out and she seemed to be getting more agitated, so we did. When we realised we couldn't get through to her, we rang you. Nothing we said worked." Shirley spoke as if she was tense, or maybe even irritated, but then her tone softened as she added, "I was worried about making things worse."

Was it just naughtiness, or is something really disturbing her I wondered? It was our job to decide. Her future depended on us.

I'd long ago learned to control the butterflies that crowded into my tummy when called to deal with difficult situations like this. They were still there, but now served only to keep me on my toes. I'd never wish such a serious trauma on anyone, but I liked the feeling that maybe I could help.

Angus continued. "What would make a young woman pace about like that? It's certainly a new one on me." He seemed puzzled too. Neither of us ventured a reply, but thinking through possible answers would help us understand Ellie.

"It's up to you now." Shirley concluded, folding her arms in front of her.

"Shall we go on in then?" Angus asked me.

"Ok." I nodded to Gus and we walked to the door of the classroom.

## CHAPTER TWO

I reached the door first, knocked, and opened it a little. I stopped in the doorway looking around. I didn't see her at first, but the pupil's world spread out before me. Everything was cheerful, the walls were decorated with colourful student pictures and jolly photos. Signs of youth were everywhere. The room was designed to be a pleasure to be in, and I guess for most students it was. But not for this particular one. I looked around me and at last saw Ellie, and I was shocked, I couldn't imagine a greater contrast.

"Hi. Is it ok to come in?" I asked the room's occupant. There was no answer. I went in anyway. Gus followed and shut the door behind us.

Now we could both see Ellie clearly. She looked a mess. What should have been a pink, healthy complexion was tinged grey, sallow and ashy. Her tangled auburn hair was held behind her in what should have been a pony tail, except that only part of it was caught in the elastic band, the rest was sticking out and falling loose. Her school tie was pulled out, her shirt collar wide open and her sleeves rolled up. Her hands were in front of her eyes a lot of the time. She was sobbing, crying, deep meaningful sobs that racked her whole body in their intensity -, she was so wrapped up in her grief she didn't even seem to notice us. She stood as if she had the weight of the world on her shoulders and almost looked like an old, wizened woman in a young person's place.

Angus and I went to the pupil's seats. We purposefully didn't sit at the teacher's desk, I didn't want us to look too teacherly and I guessed he'd had the same thought.

"Is it ok if we sit down?" Angus asked, putting three chairs in a circle, obviously hoping she'd join us. "There's a chair here for you," he said to Ellie. She didn't acknowledge us, so Gus and I sat down anyway. I kept my posture quite relaxed and informal, and kicked off my tight city shoes, to set a relaxed tone for the interview.

Ellie seemed totally self-absorbed, muttering something unintelligible and sobbing constantly. She was pacing around the room restlessly, her eyes glazed over, apparently unseeing. She punched various desks a few times, seemingly oblivious to the pain she must be feeling in her hands. Then she'd sit at a desk, folding her arms in front of her and burying her head in them, sobbing for all the world was worth before getting up and repeating the whole sorry episode again.

It didn't take me long to see that this was no play acting. This was genuine distress, terror even. We watched silently for a while. I was hoping she'd join us, but she didn't. Ellie looked straight at me, but her big brown eyes didn't seem to focus, they were flooded with tears, pleading for comfort. Her stress pulled at my heart strings and I ached that someone so young should feel so bad. Having been through emotional turmoil myself I knew just how badly it shook you to the core.

Judging by his body language, it looked to me as though Angus agreed Ellie's distress was genuine. He seemed to be like me, full of sympathy judging by his expression.

Ellie carried on as before sobbing and sobbing as if we weren't in the room. This was a cry for help if ever I saw one. It was as if she was screaming, shouting as loud as possible non-verbally, for the whole world to hear her pain, desperately hoping that someone, somewhere, would have the key to curing it for her. All we had to do was find that key.

On these sorts of occasions I usually say the least possible to give the client space to talk. But Ellie was so wrapped up in her grief she didn't even seem to know we were in the room. So I spoke to her, choosing open questions, questions that require more than a one word reply, so that they would prompt Ellie to give us detail. But first we had to establish contact and get her to acknowledge us even before we could expect her to speak.

It was Angus who broke the silence, crossing his long legs casually in front him. "Hi. We're Angus and Louise. Would you like to know why we're here?" his voice was full of compassion. We instinctively kept the tone of our voices quiet and calm. Even though we'd only just met, we'd slipped into a very easy and natural way of working together.

There was still no reply and Ellie still didn't acknowledge us, it was as if she simply didn't even know we were in the room. "We've put a chair ready for you here." Angus said again, patting the empty chair for encouragement.

She still didn't respond.

I thought I'd try. "Hi. My name's Louise and I'm a social worker. This is Angus, he's a doctor. People are really worried about you, you know. That's why they've asked us to come and see you."

Ellie slowly turned her head and looked in our direction, her gaze focused on me and her expression changed from distress to horror in a matter of seconds. "A what? A social worker? I don't need no social worker!" Her body flooded with anger, she clenched her fists till her knuckles were white. She leant towards me, totally fuming just like a toddler in a tantrum. "That is stupid!" she shouted, tears ran fast and furiously down her cheeks. She took a few steps backwards, fury totally enveloping her whole body. "What do you think you're doing here? I haven't even got no children to take away, have I!"

I was shocked by the intensity of her fury. It was as if the whole world had plotted against her. I thought it couldn't be just in response to having a social worker present and it confirmed to me my earlier thoughts that there was something seriously unpleasant happening in her life and I was seeing emotional overspill, how the feelings from one thing have spilled over into another. But what was it? I kept calm as years of experience had taught me to do.

"We do more than just take children away you know." I answered in soothing tones, pleased that she was at least talking. I believed our peaceful mood would rub off on her in time, when her fury had burnt itself out and she was ready to listen. "There's loads more to social work than just taking children away from people you know. We help sort out all sorts of problems."

We waited for Ellie's reply, but she said nothing, just stood facing away from us, crying and wiping her tears away with her fist.

Angus spoke next, his tone calm and sympathetic. "You look really upset. We're here to help you know. Sometimes it's easier to speak to someone you don't know, someone you know won't tell anyone else, someone you might not ever have to see again if you don't want to. Why don't you come and tell us what's wrong?"

There was no reply. Ellie looked away from us and paced around the room, still sobbing.

I looked over at the doctor, he looked at me. His expression mirrored my thoughts exactly. What could we do next? We'd both tried our best, and had got absolutely nowhere, just like the people who'd been here before us. But we couldn't give up, not just yet.

We sat quietly for a moment, giving her a chance to reply in her own time. She didn't for a long time, but after a while did she glance at me, for just a nanosecond. I took a chance and lightened the tone of my speech a little. I was almost running out of ideas to get her to open up and didn't know what we'd do if we got nowhere.

"I am quite good at solving problems, you know." I risked a small smile and looked straight at her., "I've done it before and met some really nice young people just like you. We've usually ended up being friends."

At last Ellie stopped pacing and looked first at me directly, then straight out of the window. Her vision seeming to engage a little more with her surroundings now. After a while she turned towards me, she picked up a textbook and flicked through it as she spoke. "Yeah, well no-one can do anything anyway. It's my problem. Mine and Nan's."

At last a response. I was overjoyed. Now to work on getting proper communication.

"Mrs McComber says your Nan's ill, is that right? Because I think that could be a big reason for feeling upset." Gus asked.

"Well, duh!" she choked out between sobs, "It's hardly going to make me happy is it?! She's got  cancer, if you must know. And a bad sort so Nan says, 'cos she told me on the phone yesterday that she can't come home yet," Ellie shouted. "But you don't know anything about my Nan, do you?!"

I worried about what sort of carer would give a young person bad news like that on the phone knowing that she had so little support at home. But I supposed Nan might have been too poorly herself to have thought about what she was doing and maybe just didn't put two and two together.

"Try me." Gus said asked, with a hint of a challenge in his voice, "You're right. I don't know anything about your Nan. But I do know about cancer, because it's in my family too."

Ellie looked straight at him, seemingly astonished, as if it had never occurred to her that anyone else could ever have cancer in their family. "But you're a doctor?" She furrowed her brow, puzzled.

Angus continued. "Cancer happens to doctors too, you know. I've had several relatives die from it. My mum died of cancer. Others in my family survived it. I felt guilty though, because as a doctor I thought I should have been able to save them. But I couldn't."

Ellie didn't respond, but looked straight at him and listened attentively. Then, after a few moments silence, she spoke, dropping her gaze and looking calmer.

"My Nan's in hospital having an operation right now." A tear ran down her cheek and, she wiped it away quickly on her shirt sleeve. "I dunno if she's gonna die or not. She was alright last week. Then she couldn't swallow right, so she went to the doctors, then she went to hospital for just a few days and now she's not allowed out and I don't know what's happening."

"That is hard for you, I totally get that." Gus creased his brow in sympathy. "It might be that nobody will know much at the moment, not even the doctors. But I can help you find out. It could be too early yet to know what sort of cancer it is and how we can treat it, but we can try."

I patted the chair next to us, inviting her to sit down. She ignored me so I let it go, I didn't want to interrupt the flow of conversation. "Maybe today wasn't a good day to come to school. Maybe you're just too tense to concentrate," I suggested.

"What else can I do?" Ellie shouted more from frustration this time, and not as though she was particularly shouting at anyone, but just to get rid of some of her tension. Tears still running furiously down her cheeks and her voice quivering. "There's no-one at home to look after me anyway. I know I'd only mope if I was anywhere else. Nan's having an operation so I can't even speak to her on the phone today. I wanted to come to school to keep me busy." She made fists which she banged on a table in frustration. "Why can't someone just tell me she'll be alright? I can't live with this worry!"

"It's the not knowing that's so hard, isn't it?' Angus said. "It's true that some people survive cancer, some don't. People can die of cancer at any age, sometimes leaving their relatives in the saddest circumstances." Angus sounded as if he was speaking from the heart too as he explained. I suspect he thought the same as me, that there was no point in lying to her because she seemed easily bright enough to work things out for herself. "I could sit here and tell you that the chances are good these days, and more people survive cancer now than used to. And that would be completely true. But that won't be much help to you because what you want to know is if your Nan is going to get better or not. Some people do die of cancer that's for sure and it might be that no-one will be able to tell you what will happen will apply to your Nan yet, especially if she is in the early stages of her illness."

Ellie stood silently, listening to Gus's every word. She was calmer now and the tears slowed up.

"Hey, come here. Come and sit down," I tried again, now that Ellie had fully engaged with us. I patted the chair next to me. Ellie stood a second as if deciding what to do then did come and sit with us. It was a great relief to see that she'd relaxed so much. "You ok?" patted her on the shoulder. She looked at me with wide open eyes like a puppy's, pleading for us to make things better. But we couldn't do that. "It's nice to have you close," I said and passed her a tissue from the packet I always kept in my bag for weeping clients. She began sobbing quietly.

Angus leant towards her, his tone soft, "Look, cancer's a big word. When it's said everyone automatically thinks of death, that whoever has got it is going to die. But in real life, lots of people do survive. Ok, there's often a period of time where there's lots going on like medical treatment, operations, chemo and stuff, and in that time it can be hard to know what the future will hold. But these days the chances are good, better than they've ever been in fact."

Ellie turned towards him and listened to his every word. She nodded in reply.

Angus continued, his tone sympathetic, "I wish I could tell you she's going to be ok, but I can't. Would you like me to find out what' is going on and let you know?"

Ellie wiped her eyes. "Yeah. S'pose." She answered.

"Tell us a bit more about your family?" I asked, puzzled, because it didn't seem to be usual, and if nnEllie was staying with friends I needed to know if she was in a safe place.

"Dunno where my dad is, I've never met him," Ellie explained without emotion, which suggested to me it was a situation she was used to. "My mum lives somewhere on the mainland. I don't see her much either. Mum won't tell me who my dad is, she never has."

"Does she know your Nan's ill?" I asked.

"Not sure. Nan couldn't get hold of her when she tried ringing. Mum wouldn't come anyway, she hates visiting the island, that's why I live with Nan. Mum says she's just not a motherly person. 'Its nuffin to do with you,' my mum said to me once, 'I'm just not like that.' We don't have any other family. There isn't anyone else that can have me."

"Some people just aren't cut out for parenting that's true." I agreed. I had seen it so often, as most social workers have. "So where are you staying whilst your Nan is in hospital?"

“With Greta and Pieter. They live just a few doors down from us. She said they’d look after me whilst Nan was in hospital. They haven’t been on the island long, they’re here while Pieter helps build the new bridge, then they’ll move on to the next job, Pieter told me.”

“Poor you,” I said sympathetically. It seemed her Nan was the only constant person in Ellie’s life, and now she was very ill. “No wonder you’re having trouble concentrating.”

I could fully understand why she was so upset. Gus did too, judging by the way he was speaking to her. I didn’t think there was any sign of mental illness or suicide in Ellie as long as what she said was true. I’d speak to the people around her later and check that, but for the meantime I gave her the benefit of the doubt.

"You have a very sad story," Gus agreed. "I think, and we’ll ask if Louise agrees, what you need now is rest.” He suggested, “I’ll call and see you at home in the next few days. That'll give me a chance to check out exactly what’s is happening with your Nan, then I can let you know."

Ellie nodded.

“That sounds like a good idea. You must be shattered,” I said to Ellie.

She sat back in her chair. The huge sobs had gone, now replaced with little sniffles. She mopped her eyes with a tissue. There was little trace of her former tension. I didn’t feel she was at any risk of suicide so long as she had support to help her through these difficult times.

"Being upset and worried is hard work. It'll make you physically tired." I explained. "But at least I can come and see you and sort out your plans and talk to Nan, so we know really what we're dealing with. Problems are a lot easier to deal with when you know exactly what's going on and what the choices are."

"Ok," Ellie agreed, looking tired. She pointed to the door. "I can see Greta now."

I saw the figures Ellie spoke of through the frosted glass, and beckoned Mrs McComber and the other lady in.

"Hello, I .... Greta." The figure from the other side of the door introduced herself hesitantly, unsure of her words. They seemed foreign to her and the accent soon confirmed she wasn't speaking in her native tongue. She walked up to Ellie and put her arm around her shoulder, "You... sad." She seemed very kind and Ellie went to her without hesitation. It didn't sound as if her English was very good though. It must be frustrating for Ellie, who needed to talk about her worries, to have a carer who, though she appeared kind and caring, couldn't quite understand what was going on or reply in any detail.

We told her with lots of hand gestures our plan for Ellie.

It must be awful for Ellie, I thought, because even something which most people take for granted like family, was uncertain for her. She must have already felt like she lost one home when her mother wouldn't or couldn't look after her, and now she wouldn't know if her Nan would be alive to continue to give her a home either. Her birth parents didn't seem to be up to the job and presumably her neighbours couldn't offer a permanent home should she need one. No wonder Ellie struggled to cope bearing that alone.

"I'll come and see you later this week," I said to Ellie, hoping that my new boss would be happy for me to do this. "You look after yourself, won't you?" It was usually considered good practice for a social worker to finish the task they'd started with a family, though sometimes managers needed someone else to take a task on. I took a chance saying I'd see her again, but since I'd had such troubles getting Ellie to confide in me there were good reasons for me to keep working with her and I thought I'd probably be allowed to. Greta and Ellie left us and the teachers thanked us for our help and went back to work.

Angus and I left together.

"Phew!" I said to him as we left the building. We had slipped immediately into a comfortable way of working together a bit like putting on a pair of old shoes. I turned to face him as, he stopped briefly. "What a way to start a new job! Who said rural social work was a doddle?" But at least work was going to be exciting. I liked that.

"Ach, you'll soon learn there's nothing about rural work that's easy, whether you're in town or country this job certainly keeps you on your toes!" Angus smiled as he returned to his car., "I'll find out what I can about the medical condition. Maybe it's not as bad as she thinks. Pop into my office later and I'll let you know." He held up his hand high to say goodbye as he walked towards his car.

“Will do,” I replied.

It did seem a possibility Ellie’s Nan might die if Ellie had understood it correctly. But you can help people to cope with whatever comes along. And the emotional rewards of helping people through such difficult times are huge.

It’s so much easier to be Louise the big clever social worker who can rescue people from difficult situations, rescue them even from themselves. But it was the Louise outside work that I should have worried about. The Louise who had messed up her own private life, the Louise who didn’t even know who she was, Louise who is now all on her own. That’s the Louise that frightens me, the person I don’t even know.

## CHAPTER THREE

I drove back to work but it was hard to drive with any speed. The surroundings were beautiful and filled me with delight. The road ambled around large open bays where sapphire blue sea met ice white sand. The beaches were dotted with granite rocks which often proved a useful perch for seabirds. I jumped once or twice when I thought I saw a rock move only to realise it was a seal just woken from slumber.

The land between the bays was mostly spreading valleys or glens dotted with hills and small mountains. Often the valleys were totally empty save for a few craggy hillocks and some wiry old hill sheep. Sometimes there was an old croft in the valley, made from the same stone as the hills surrounding it, the quartz in its rocks gleaming in the morning sunlight. I guessed the few people that lived there were all that could be classed as population. The silence and space soothed my troubled spirit in a way I struggled to understand. Maybe understanding wasn't necessary, maybe that's where I was going wrong. Maybe I should just accept things as they are and just let them be.

It was just the sort of tonic I needed after what seemed like an eternity of emotional wrangling.

Pretty soon I recognised the road in front of me as the route to my new office. I drove to the surgery which lay tucked snugly in a modern estate and pulled into the car park preparing myself for my new life. This would be my place of work for the next six months and the thought filled me with pleasure. It was totally different to what I'd been used to. Unlike the large city- centre council offices in Edinburgh of my previous post, this was a small, two-storey building, one end used as a GP's surgery, the other as the social work department.

I pressed a bell at reception, introduced myself and was taken through to the staff area.

"Lovely to see you, Louise. I hope you had a good journey." The receptionist greeted, remembering me from my interview.

I heard and recognised Janet, the Team Manager, instantly in her polo- neck jumper and tweed skirt, her long iron grey hair plaited behind her, her briskly efficient manner evident in her voice. Although I'd only met her at my interview, I found her reassuring. I thought she would be a great team manager, likely to be always calm and professional, always with the same clear, analytical thinking. I thought she'd be was too cool- headed to ever get mixed up with the wrong guy like I had, but I also felt that she would be very understanding and not at all judgemental of anyone who did. Like me.

I shuddered.

"I'm sure you remember me, don't you?" She held out her hand and shook mine firmly, "Janet Donaldson, Team Manager here. I'm so sorry we had to send you out on an emergency so quickly, but we just didn't have enough staff here qualified to work in mental health."

"That's no problem, Janet. I like getting stuck in straight away," I replied. I didn't like to say that it's easier to deal with other people's problems than my own and I'd been quite happy to be distracted from any personal thoughts that might stray into my mind.

She beckoned me to follow her and we stepped towards a smaller office. She stood aside in the doorway so that I could see inside. "Sadly there are few of us here we're always short staffed, but this is the room where the social workers sit. It's not everyone's choice of a place to live, I think. That is why we're always struggling to fill posts." She explained as she looked around the sparse room to make her point.

"I see what you mean." I followed her gaze, three of the four desks looked empty. A young woman was alone in the office and sat at one of the desks. She had a friendly face and was on the phone, waving hello to me as she spoke without interrupting her call. I guessed she was another social worker. I couldn't help but notice her bright red hair and red jumper and thought she seeemed quite lively and outgoing.

"In fact you can sit in this room if you like, the good thing is you can have your pick of these desks. How about have this one?" Janet walked towards a desk that was near a window. "It's got a lovely view and it's quite near the kettle."

"It looks fine to me." I put my coat and bags on it and looked around. It was a light, bright and cheerful room. You could see acres of sky rather than just snippets between houses like you did in the city. It felt friendly, like a second home. I knew I'd enjoy being here.

The occupant of the other desk put her phone down and stood up to join us. She had a bouncy way of moving as if she had energy in shedloads. “Hello there!” she called to me before turning to Janet, “You're slipping Janet,” she laughed and walked towards us holding out two empty cups. “Do I see that you haven’t even offered our new friend a drink?! I don't think anyone should be making their first cup of tea on their first day.” She tut-tutted to Janet in mock shame. She lifted the two cups in the air and jangled them towards me as she spoke, “Welcome. I'm Fiona. Call me Fi, another social worker and your new colleague. Tea or coffee?" She seemed chirpy and fun, yet was probably level- headed as you had to be to be a social worker. I liked her.

Janet laughed. "As you can see, the staff here keep me on my toes."

"I'm Jill," an older lady walked towards us, holding a tin of cakes and biscuits. "I'm a receptionist here and it’s my job to show you round later. But first, something more important. We like to look after ourselves so we take turns to bring in the cakes." She opened the tin and held it towards me. It was full of tasty treats.

"Oh, you found out my big weakness already!" I laughed, dipping my hand into the tin. I took a large chocolate biscuit, holding it up like treasure. "My favourite!"

"They’re my favourite too!" Fi smiled. "They make coming to work a treat don’t they? Oh before I forget, you must come to our office party next week, it’s in The Ferry Hotel, not too far away.”

“A....party?” The suggestion surprised me. I must have looked puzzled. I felt my face drain of colour and I felt shocked.

"Yes, a party. You'll find quite a lively social life on the islands. Drummond Moor is especially friendly." Janet explained, picking up on my perplexed expression. "People come here expecting it to be quiet, but quiet it is not. It's a friendly place and there's always a lot going on."

"Yeah," chimed Fi, "it's the classic thing. People come here following the end of a love affair or something like that expecting to wallow in their tragedy. But more often than that they find the islands work a kind of magic on them and they end up staying and totally changing their lives for the better."

I stood dumbfounded and tried to keep my cool. They had just summed up my reason for being here. I wondered if I had the word 'reject' or something like it written on my forehead. How did they know? But I said nothing of it and hoped the thumping of my heart didn't show.

"Janet, you're needed on the phone." A shout from a distant voice summoned Janet away.

She looked from one to the other of us, smiling goodbye. "If you'll excuse me, I'm expecting a call."

I smiled back in return. I liked the office and thought fate had led me to a place that would be good for me.

I had the map spread out over the passenger seat as I drove to the cottage that would be mine whilst I was here. Even the map looked very different to those I was used to. It had huge swathes of colour all over it. The high ground was picked out in different shades of amber showing the height of the land around me. On the journey home there was so much high ground that the whole page almost seemed to glow orange.

The sea also accounted for the vivid swathes of colour on the map and was never far away on my journey. The twisting road to the cottage seemed never ending and took me high up craggy hills and down again. But after too many twists and turns to count, a little white cottage stood out, part of the way up a hill at the end of the bay and at the foot of some rocky crags. It looked just like the photos I'd seen of the place and was miles from anywhere. Well, I guess I did tell the agency that I wanted somewhere isolated, I reminded myself. I hadn't had time to view the house before I agreed to rent it. They'd certainly found me somewhere remote.

I stopped and looked at it from afar, taking in every detail. It almost looked like two sugar cubes joined together except that it had a little cheerful red front door in the middle and windows each side. None of the walls were straight, they had the bumpy appearance of something that had been hand made. The roof was thatched and came down so low I thought I'd almost be able to touch it without stretching. At the front of the house was a garden bench that overlooked the bay. 'That's somewhere to sit and have your breakfast every morning,' I told myself. It was gorgeous. Just what I'd hoped for.

The place was every bit as lovely inside. Downstairs there were two rooms. A huge rustic fireplace dominated the sitting room which made it looked really cosy, a squashy sofa and a couple of old arm chairs completed the look. There was also a little kitchen, small but with everything I'd need. Upstairs there were two tiny bedrooms, one with an old brass bed and a couple of old chests of drawers and a wardrobe, the other with a single bed and chest of drawers. A tiny bathroom was squashed in beside the smaller bedroom. There were no carpets anywhere, just bare floorboards, which made the house look very rustic. I felt the Spartan look suited my mood at the moment. I had instinctively pared back to just the basics. I'd needed to get away from Simon and his plush lifestyle with every mod con and lavish spending. This felt more me and I looked forward to living here.

It might only be just a little house, but it seemed to me it breathed a welcome especially for me. For the next few months at least it was all mine, I had total control over what went on within its walls. It was my safe haven, my little castle. It might not match up to the grandeur and space of Simon's chic, city centre apartment with its minimalist modern décor, big stone wall and electric gates, but the cottage felt safe, as if all the people who had once lived there were kindred spirits and had left their traces in the old walls to watch over me.

The windows in the house were deeply buried inside the ancient stone walls. They might be small, but through them on the front side of the house you could see the whole panorama of the bay, and beyond that the distant hills of another island. There was a teeny harbour with boats busily going about their business far beneath me, whilst others bobbed about on the surface tied to their moorings.

I got myself some supper then ran myself a hot bath using my best bath oil. I sank into the hot, scented water and let the feeling of bliss warm me through to my bones. I stretched my arms and legs out in the warm water. It struck me that I was also stretching myself out to my new life. My new life alone. I hadn't really ever been single before. The feeling was unnatural, raw, scary, exciting.

It had taken a long time to break out of the emotional trap that my life in Edinburgh had become. But now it was like learning to breathe for the first time. There had seemed to be nothing I could do in Edinburgh to stop bumping into all Simon's friends, or passing the places Simon and I used to go. I forgot how many times his friends had spoken to me astonished that I had given up such a 'nice' partner and such a plush lifestyle. They just didn't get that I'm really not into money, no matter how hard I explained. But as I sank into the water the cloying memory of Simon, his lifestyle and his dominating tactics it began to feel like yesterday and I felt as though a noose around my neck was starting to loosen.

I smiled remembering how one of my friends had explained my predicament. "The trouble with you is you didn't choose your relationship, you fell into it," she had said to me. And they were right. I guess this is the typical social worker's dilemma, you always see the good in people, even when it is mixed with bad. And I sure had spent a lot of time excusing Simon's bad behaviour.

It took a long time until I could see that I had to get out. And now I had to learn to live my life all over again, this time all on my own. I had seen the same terror in Ellie's eyes, the same gut wrenching horror that I felt when I first realised I was alone, as she may soon be soon. Despite the trappings of respectability, house, car, holiday home, Simon and I weren't really an item. I was just one of Simon's toys, a young trophy object to be brought out when needed and discarded when not wanted and ignored otherwise. It had taken me years first to get the courage to leave him then to rid myself of his web of control. But now I had.

## CHAPTER FOUR

There hadn't been a day since I met Ellie that I haven't thought of her and the difficult situation she's in. If her Nan died, where would she go if her parents weren't up to caring for her? Her future was not clear and if we were to avoid any further anxiety attacks from her I knew I had to understand the what was happening  in order to help her come to terms with it. I had to ask another social worker to check out the people who had been looking after her to ensure they were safe. That would be done by another social worker in case of conflict of interests. It would be their job to start the police checks and assessment necessary to check that the home and carers were suitable for her.

I pulled up outside the house Ellie was staying at without an appointment so I could meet her and the people she was staying with and find out more about her in the half hour or so we had until Ellie would arrive home from school. Not having an appointment would give me the chance to see how they really lived, they wouldn't be able to clean or tidy especially for me.

The house stood in a terrace of modern houses in a little village.

I pressed the doorbell.

The door opened promptly. "Oh, hi." The speaker was Greta, I recognised her from the school, was a woman in her mid-thirties with shoulder length brown hair and a foreign accent. She smiled at me in recognition but her expression quickly changed to concern. She tried to speak to me but her English faltered too much for conversation. "In .......... In ....." she indicated for me to follow her in and called to someone upstairs in a language I didn't recognise.

"Thank you," I replied, worried as to what I was about to hear. What if she were to tell me they couldn't keep Ellie any longer? Where could she go then?

We went through the sitting room which was spotlessly clean. A warm fire glowed in the hearth and the smell of something savoury cooking, maybe a casserole, floated in from the kitchen. She gestured me to take a seat. I did so. "I just wanted to talk to you about Ellie, then see Ellie when she's home from school," I explained. I don't think she understood a word, but she smiled politely.

Someone in heavy boots was coming downstairs. Greta tapped her wedding ring and pointed to explain he was her husband. I smiled in approval.

Then she tapped her watch. ".......Ellie ........ Ellie," she said, pointing to her watch face to indicate that Ellie would be back soon.

I nodded in understanding.

"Er ..... kaffe...?" Greta asked hesitantly.

I guessed she meant coffee. "That would be lovely, thank you." I followed her into the kitchen. I'd wanted to see if it was suitable for a young person. Was plenty of good food about? Was it safe for a young person? What about cleanliness and hygiene? It looked pleasingly clean, neat and tidy. Some framed photographs were displayed on a shelf. A calendar was pinned to the wall and looked full of what looked like appointments all written in a different language. I took it as a sign that this was a well- organised house and if Ellie were to need any medical appointments, they would be kept. That isn't always the case in my line of work, and it gave me confidence that this was a family that valued input from professionals.

Greta sat opposite me, directly facing me as if she had nothing to hide. But there was something clearly worrying her. She grimaced and sat twisting her wedding ring round and round her finger. If the reason for her worry hadn't come out by the end of the interview, I'd have to ask her directly, but for now I let it rest.

I wanted to know what sort of people Greta and her husband were and how they were dealing with Ellie, especially if she was as difficult at home as she had been at school. Fortunately we were joined at that point by Greta's husband. "Hello," he said in a deep voice with foreign overtones but clearly understandable. "Pieter Tyzak, Greta's husband." He thrust his hand at me to shake. "Welcome."

Greta said something to him that he understood, judging by the context, she was probably explaining who I was.

He joined us in the kitchen. He towered over me by at least nine inches and wore the clothes of a working man, blue cotton overalls and heavy worker's boots. He had a lovely, big warm smile, a single gold ring earing in one ear, and a kind face topped with a thatch of dark blonde hair.

Greta put the coffees on a tray and said something in her own language. Pieter in his better English even though it still wasn't perfect, he said that we should follow Greta into the sitting room.

I sat in a chair by the fire and explained the purpose of my visit. "Because you're looking after someone not related to either of you, we need to do an assessment of you so that we can be sure Ellie is safe here, not that we suspect that you're not good parents, but that we can offer help if need be before things get to boiling point."

"Yah, yah," Pieter agreed, explaining things to his wife. "Sure. We both say you come here anytime," he said to me. "We hide nothing."

I used the first part of the interview to discover some more about the couple's history. Greta didn't always understand and Pieter had to translate, but we got there in the end. It seemed they had recently moved from Poland and both Greta and her husband Pieter had come from big families so were quite used to children and young people.

I had to ask how long they could have Ellie for but the time didn't seem right straight away.

"Ellie not easy you know, my wife says" Pieter explained, and he translated what Greta was telling him. "She get upset often. She spend time in her room alone. She talk to no-one. We go and ask her if she alright, but she say yes. And she still cries."

Greta looked relieved as Pieter explained what had been bothering her.

"Was she like that before she came to live here?" I asked. That would be a useful guide to see how her circumstances were affecting her.

"I don't think she was particularly quiet at home, not that I know her that well," Pieter answered in consultation with his wife.

"Well, if you don't know her that well, how did she come to be here?" I asked, anyone taking in a child without having been vetted by Social Services rang alarm bells in me. No-one had checked their motives or whether they were offering safe and caring homes up until now. So often the opposite was true.

"Her Nan live a few doors along," Pieter pointed with his fingers where he lacked words. "Greta always look for work when new town, but nothing here, so she do cleaning for Nan. Then she ask me if I have Ellie while in hospital. Nan says they has no other family."

"How long is Nan going to be in?" I asked. It might be ok for Ellie to stay here a few days, a week or so, but hopefully it wouldn't be for long. There seemed to be no plans for what would happen if Greta couldn't have her any more or wanted to take a job.

"We don't know," Pieter shrugged his shoulders. "They problems for Nan. We see her and she not well. More lump, how you say? Bigger and badder. Might not get better."

My stomach did a somersault. I know it wasn't confirmed yet, but the signs weren't good.

"Does Ellie know?" I asked. No wonder Ellie was finding her worries too much to cope with when she was at school.

"Yes. Yes, Nan tell her." Greta looked very concerned, understandably and struggled to speak to me in my language. This was clearly what had been worrying her earlier. "She don't speak much to me. Maybe my English?" She supplemented her words with a shrug of her shoulders and a few hand gestures.

I warmed to this lady. She cared. I didn't think there was anything sinister here. She and her husband had taken in a young woman they barely knew and I felt they were trying to do their best for her.

"It's good that she can stay here and that you can take her to see her grandmother. How long can she stay with you here?" I had asked the million dollar question. I dreaded their answer.

"Not long." Pieter explained. "Months maybe. I work building new bridge." He pointed in that direction. "It nearly finish. Then we move to next job."

I felt my stomach go cold. I didn't speak straight away.

Pieter continued. "That's what job is. We go anywhere contracts take us. We save to buy house in our country."

I could hardly believe what I was hearing. I had to check that I had heard right. "Ellie won't be able to stay here long?" I asked. How could life be so cruel to such a nice young woman as Ellie?

“No.” The couple answered in unison, their expressions clearly showing they were just as worried about Ellie’s future as I was.

“Ok,” I nodded, ignoring the lump in my throat. As I spoke Ellie came in the house.

We spent a few minutes greeting Ellie, who looked pleased to see me. Greta got her a drink and biscuit and we went her up to her room so I could speak to her in private. She dumped her bag down on the bed with a ‘couldn’t care less’ attitude and sat down. She turned to face me but her gaze never looked up, it stayed solemnly down. I could see she was fighting back tears.

“So how’s you?” I asked, using an open question so she could tell me what she liked in her own time.

She didn’t. She just shrugged her shoulders. I should have known by now that she needed a bit of drawing out in conversation. I tried again. “How was school, did you have a nice day?” I asked.

She sat at the top of the bed, legs wrapped up around her, picking split ends off her hair. “S’pose.” She answered, without giving me eye contact.

I persevered with open questions. “Have you heard from your Nan lately?”

She nodded in response.

“How is she?” I asked. Judging by Ellie’s manner I already guessed the answer.

"Bad." Ellie replied, her eyes welling up with tears. "She still thinks she's going to die."

I wished her Nan could give her a cheerful message sometimes, but I suppose being so ill made her not think about the effect on Ellie of what she said. I reached over and held her hands. "That might be just how she feels now. It might not be what actually happens. Dr Angus said they haven't got the results of all the tests back yet so they don't know for sure."

Her tears dropped onto my hand. I reached over and passed her a tissue. "Look," I implored, unable to stop feeling heartbroken for her myself. "Let's face that if it comes to it, not before, eh?" I squeezed her hands harder. "There's no harm in thinking of other places you could live but remember it might not actually come to that."

"We haven't got any one else in our family." Ellie answered. As soon as she wiped one tear away it was replaced by another. "The only other person I can think of is someone I've never met."

"Who's that, sweet?" I asked, setting my hopes high.

"My dad." Ellie said between sobs. "My mum will never tell me who he is, but I will have a dad. I don't even think mum's told him I exist. But when he finds out he'll surely want me?"

Phew. I took a deep breath and tried to keep my cool. I knew only too well the reality of that statement. Men who find out they have children they don't know about don't always relish the thought of being a parent. It could be that there were very good reasons why her mother didn't tell him about her. Or maybe he did know about her and didn't want to know.

Judging by her tone Ellie was hoping for a happy ever after outcome with her dad if her Nan died. I thought it was like clutching at straws, grasping for the unknown. But should I let her keep believing her fantasy? Should I tell her what I thought, even if it totally deflated her? I opted for a middle course. "There are too many unknowns," I explained in an attempt to let her down lightly. "We'll put together our options when we're sure we know how Nan is."

"... k ...." Ellie wiped her tears again.

Greta knocked on the door to ask about dinner and, seeing Ellie in such distress, she came in., "Oh, look," she said kindly, stroking her hand down the side of Ellie's face and leaning towards her. Ellie leant sideways into Greta's shoulder and cried some more. Greta hugged her close, whispering to her in soothing tones in her native language. It was a lovely, caring and sensitive thing to do and made me realise what a kind couple they seemed to be and how lucky Ellie was to find them.

But whatever luck she had been having now looked like it would soon be running out and Ellie may well have nowhere to live and no-one in her life. I had to meet her Nan and ask her what options there would be for Ellie if Nan she was to die. Leaving Ellie in Greta's capable hands, I said my goodbyes and promised to come back soon.

## CHAPTER FIVE

It was later that week that I had my first child protection visit on the island. I was on duty so it was my turn to deal with any random office visits and calls that day. You just never know who's going to be on the end of the phone when you pick it up when you're on duty. I like the challenge, whatever comes in it's down to me. It's unpredictable and exciting. The phone went just as I came back from lunch. I picked it up and said in a crisp, business-like manner, "social services here, can I help you?"

"Hello. I'm Felicity Passmore, one of the Health Visitors here," the voice on the other end of the phone announced. She sounded very calm and collected. "I've just been to see a family and I wasn't very happy with the way a child is treated. The older child had been slapped and I wanted you to know."

Adrenaline flooded into my veins as it always did when hearing about children at risk. I prepared to take full details. "Okay then, I'll just get my notepad," I gathered paper and pen, "carry on then."

Felicity waited patiently until I was ready then began explaining. Then she began. "The family I have just been to see are mum Clare Singleton and her children, Joe, age seven, and baby Tom. Clare has been a single parent to Joe all his life but recently she's teamed up with a chap called Connor Crossley. Connor moved here from the mainland to help build the bridge but met up with Clare and Joe and moved in with them about a year ago. They've got a new baby, Tom, who is six weeks old. That's why I'm involved." I knew the routine pretty well, as did Felicity, so I trotted out the questions and she trotted out the answers and we got maximum information in minimum time.

"How old are the parents, do you know?" We began to rattle through the referral briskly, like professionals who had done this hundreds of times, as we both had.

"Clare is 24, Connor is 26." Felicity proceeded to read the family's dates of birth to me. I jotted them down quickly.

"So what were you unhappy about?" I asked, and paused, giving her every opportunity to tell me everything, my pen poised above the paper, ready to make notes that are essential as so many cases are very complex and have many family members.

Felicity cleared her throat. "I went to visit the family this morning," she explained, "It was part of a routine visit as I was just passing. When I went in Joe, he's seven, was looking rather sad and tearful. I asked him what was wrong, he said Connor hit him. Obviously I was instantly concerned, that is no way to treat a child."

"Was he hurt at all?" Butterflies jiggled in my stomach. I hated the thought of such a young child being hurt by someone so much bigger than him. But on the other hand you had to bear in mind that it could just be a one-off incident and it wouldn't happen again. Getting too tense about it could lead to us taking the child away and causing a lot of damage when a different approach would work best. It was always a difficult judgement to make and one that often caused me and many other social workers sleepless nights.

"I looked at Joe's arm," Felicity continued. "There was a red mark in the shape of a slap. I insisted on taking him into the bedroom so that I could look at him all over and ask him when he was on his own to tell me what had happened."

"Were the family ok about that? Did they try to deny it?" I asked.

"Connor is stepfather and he was very cross. He called me an interfering bitch and shouted at me. He insisted it was just a wee smack because he wouldn't eat his porridge. I wouldn't be surprised if he made a habit of it, he seemed a bit rough and blasé about Joe. Clare said she wasn't in the room at the time. I didn't feel there was any risk to me, it's not the professionals he'd hurt, I thought Connor's talk was all just bluster. But I am worried about the children. I felt Connor was young and out of his depth, and it's obviously not acceptable to hit children."

"What did Joe say in the bedroom?" I queried, the human part of me dreading the answer, the professional in me was saying at least we could change things in his life from now on, the feeling part of me recognising every single inch of the pain.

"Joe doesn't like Connor. Mum was changing the baby's nappy in a bedroom so she didn't see, but Joe said Connor kept on and on, telling Joe to eat every last scrap of his meal. When Joe refused for the umpteenth time and flicked the porridge across the room, Connor slapped his upper arm. It is okay, I don't think he needs any medical treatment but I'm worried about the tension in the family. There was a feeling in the house that things weren't right, nobody was giving anybody else eye contact and there was a kind of hesitancy about them, as if they'd just had an argument and the stress and tension was still hanging in the air."

"I know what you mean," I acknowledged. "Did you tell them you're are going to involve social services?"

"I did. I said they should expect a social worker, and probably police, calling. That didn't go down well either, Connor insisted he sees the problem now and didn't want me to tell you. They were both very worried about that and didn't want social workers involved. But I explained it's about giving them help to make sure it doesn't happen again, not necessarily taking the children away. They said that they were busy, going out and wouldn't be here for a social workers call, so I reminded them that what they had done was very serious and they needed to deal with it otherwise the children might be better off in care. They changed their minds then, and agreed to be in when you visit."

"Anything else?" I asked, smiling at Felicity's tactics.

"I explained that we'll need to have a child protection conference but that we will probably be working together to try and keep children at home with their parents. I wouldn't want to see the children taken away from them, but I really think Connor needs to grow up and learn a more mature way to deal with what he's taken on if he's going to continue in that family – or any family for that matter."

"I quite agree, it sounds like they might just need help to learn other ways of managing children. Thanks for that, Felicity," I said, scribbling in the last the details down on my pad, "I'll just go and have a word with Janet and speak to you again. It was my job to tell the manager about any child protection issues so that she could talk through with me and the child protection police and agree what needed to be done. There are clear procedures to be followed anytime a child at risk is bought to our attention and it starts with telling a manager, which can be easy to miss when you're busy. It's easy to get so hyped up that you miss things, so often the best thing to do it put the kettle on, have a cup of tea and plan in the team with a manager in a relaxed way. It's also about getting the evidence right, in case any court case comes out of it at some future point.

Luckily for me there was already a policeman from the Police Child Protection Team in the office talking to Janet. She asked him to come and speak to me before he left.

Minutes later he stood before me, tall and slim in a neat grey suit, (child protection officers don't wear uniform) with cropped pale hair framing an angular face.  He was very tall and slim and had an air of confidence about him. He didn't look the island type at all, although he was very handsome in a modern, city kind of way.

"Vince Butler." He introduced himself with a broad smile and sturdy handshake, "Police Child Protection Unit Officer. You've got a case and you'd like one of our team to work on with you I understand?"

"Oh yes, that's right." I told him all about it and he asked some sensible questions. It was often a pleasure to work with the police in child protection. Some report recommended it years ago since child abuse is also a crime, and this chap seemed very nice. Sort of calm and capable, with a professional, confident air about him.

"I'll just get the office to do a check on Connor," he said, clicking through his mobile phone. "To see if he's got any previous for violence, drugs or anything. I'll check if the interview suite is free later too."

"Good idea," I replied. Now I could reassure Janet when we spoke to her that this was done before we sat down to plan where, how and when we were going to see this family.

Past history could tell us if we might be dealing with sophisticated abusers who were part of a ring, but it can only tell you so much because there's always a first time. "No, no previous on him," Vince said as he put the phone down.

"Good. Shall we go and see Janet together to plan how best to keep this child safe?" I said. It looked to me like it was probably a question of a joint visit between a social worker and child protection police, but there are times when a different approach is needed, depending on each situation, and Janet was the person to discuss that with. It is quite easy to think you know what to do and how to do it, so it helps to have someone else to talk the case through with.

I knocked on Janet's office door and she called us in. She knew what we needed to talk about. I went through the details with both Janet and Vince, it was a strategy meeting to find out what had actually happened and plan to keep the children safe.

Vince and I sat on the edge of our chairs, unwittingly displaying the inevitable tension. “I have checked with our office,” Vince announced with authority, “There’ is no previous history on either Clare or Connor.”

Janet sat back in her chair, arms crossed in front of her, and went through the possible outcomes with us. “At least since he’s got no previous history it sounds as if he won’t be a threat to you two when you visit.” Staff safety was always a concern with good managers, it can obviously be very dangerous to meet anyone in their own home, especially in what was likely to be tense circumstances. “If it is just Connor’s lack of experience in looking after children we can get some outreach work to help him to learn better ways of managing children. If not we’ll have to speak to Clare about safety. It might be best if Connor left the house if he won’t work with us, we can’t leave either boy in danger like that.”

“Yes,” I agreed, “a lot depends on exactly how violent he is and how keen he is to work with us.

Janet agreed we needed a joint visit straightaway. "Can you could both go out now? I'll get someone else to cover duty for you, Louise." She looked from one to the other of us.

"Thanks, Janet." I looked over at Vince, "I’m free if you’re free?"

“Fine by me.” Vince suggested, “I think we need to interview Joe in the interview suite, I know we haven’t got much to go on in the referral, but we don't know how often Connor's hit Joe before."

"Point taken." Janet and I agreed, meaning that a chat in the bedroom wouldn't be enough. We'd need a special interview in the interview suite the police used for victims of rape, abuse and that sort of thing.

A few minutes later that we were in an unmarked police car on our way.

"Are you new to the island?" Vince asked as he sat back in the seat. He had a particularly competent way of driving, chin high, hands at the bottom of the steering wheel just moving it slightly as we travelled, yet he guided the car expertly around the bends. Very swish, and maybe slightly arrogant, I thought.

"I am," I replied abruptly. I wasn't keen on talking about my private life with anyone, so I decided I'd answer his questions quite simply, giving neither more nor less information than necessary. "I'm just here for six months, then I go back to my Edinburgh post."

"Really? You live there?" He looked round at me. I nodded.

"You're not far away from me then." He looked around at me, pleased at the co-incidence. "I usually work in the Borders. I'm here on a short secondment too. I'll be going back to my usual post there myself in the next few months."

I nodded but didn't respond. If his smile was meant as an introduction to a pally chat about living near each other, he wasn't going to get it. He didn't give up easy though.

He turned towards me, I could sense his eyes looking directly at me even though I kept looking straight ahead. "What brings you to the island?"

I turned to face my passenger window. "I just wanted to try island living for a short while."

His reply next question was more direct, obviously hunting for information about my private life. "Are you like me, escaping from a bad relationship? That seems to me to be a pretty common reason for moving here, well, in the police force anyway."

I was a bit miffed by his intrusive questions, so I didn't answer in detail. "I suppose for me it's just time in life to explore new things," is how I replied. I liked him but wasn't being pushed into giving more away about me than I wanted. Not yet anyway.

So I changed the subject entirely. "Oh, look over there! How cute." I pointed out a delightful house something like my own, a tiny cottage on a lone hill, surrounded by sheep and a quaint little old washing line with aprons, tea cloths and towels on it. The windows shone bright and clean, hens picked at the rocky soil in the garden. I wouldn't have recognised it at the time but that house, and even Vince in his sophisticated, city-type way were assuring me that real life after Simon did exist and the island was working its magic and healing my heart like balm dripping on an open wound.

Vince took the hint this time. He didn't seem to see the charm of the little cottage and missed it on purpose I thought. As I got to know him better I saw his style was modern city minimalism. I reckon in his book pretty cottages are strictly for weekends and holidays and only then with a crate of the right sort of wine. I kept the chat to work topics after that.

Pretty soon we found our destination. We parked the car in the car park meant for the small, social housing estate. For the most part the houses were neat and tidy with plentiful signs of homeliness, neatly planted gardens and furnished with tables and chairs. But a glance at the whole row of houses soon confirmed which was our destination. As is often the case, the one we were to visit was the most run down and dirty house in the group.

## CHAPTER SIX

The garden was a jungle of overgrown grass and ivy, littered with junk. An old, broken pushchair, rusty and covered with bindweed, stood to one side. A couple of black bags full of rubbish were piled up and splitting at the sides. Little puddles in the plastic showed me they'd been there some time. A concrete path led from gate to door. It was cracked, each crack populated with grass and weeds, so that there was barely any difference between it and what looked like it was supposed to be a lawn.

A grubby net curtains hung at the windows, their task irrelevant as the windows were so grimy. I walked in front of Vince up the garden path, picking my way between broken paving and watching my heels didn't get stuck in the gaps.

The front door was liberally dredged with dirt, which was at its thickest by the handle and doorbell. I chose the cleanest part of the doorbell and confidently pushed it until I heard it ring indoors. We stood for a minute in the biting cold wind. A net curtain twitched and voices could be heard within. Despite trying, I couldn't make out what they were saying, but their tone was angry.

You never know exactly what to expect in this situation. It could be a mouthful of abuse, screaming and shouting, or deadly silence. This is the daily bread and butter of child protection social work. Whatever you're faced with there can be only one response. You need to be calm whatever the costs, in order to get the most aggressive of people peaceful enough so that they'll work with you to make any changes necessary for the welfare of the children. It's not easy, but it is rewarding.

After an overlong pause the door was opened by a young woman, who I guessed she was Clare. She wasn't very tall but her ample frame more than filled her jeans, which were criss-crossed here and there with fashionable rips and tears. Cold white flesh spilled over the waistband, the seams were stretched to breaking point. It was impossible to imagine how she got them on, unless she had been poured into them.

Her hair was dyed a bright shade of chemical red at the bottom fading to deep brown at the top, the two shades clashing in their quest for dominance. Her pallor was testament to an unhealthy lifestyle. She looked at us through black- rimmed eyes and said "Yeah?" with an indifferent groan.

"Hello," I held my identification card up in front of her, Vince did likewise. "I'm Louise Kimber, social worker, and this is my colleague Vince Butler from the police child protection unit. I wondered if we could come in and have a chat please?"

She looked from one to the other of us, and at our identification cards. A flash of anger flicked across her expression. She turned her back on us at the same time as muttering, "You'd betta' come in then." Her voice was whisper quiet, and monotone.

We followed her along a corridor, a smell of old cooking, nappies and body odour overwhelmed us the further we got into the house. My first impressions were just as I expected, inside was just as bad as outside. We stepped over more black bags full of rubbish and piles of washing, some clean, some looking like it was probably dirty as far as I could see.

She gestured us to go into the sitting room. As walked in I glanced around. There was no carpet on the stairs, the walls which must once have been painted white, were now splashed and grubby. Baby things were littered everywhere, a bottle of medicine with the spoon used to give it was dumped on the table in easy reach of a child, dirty plates and bowls were spread on every horizontal surface. The baby was wide awake in his pushchair, not particularly looking at anything, just sitting quietly.

A young man, probably Connor, sat on the sofa drinking something from a can and watching sport on the television, an overflowing ashtray nearby. He sat as close to the TV as possible without getting inside it, totally engrossed with the sport. I saw it was a can of energy drink he was drinking. He had multiple piercings on his ears and scratched, self-made tattoos on his arms. He took no notice of us when we entered the room, and noisily cheered on his team, apparently totally unaware of us. There was no sign of seven year old Joe.

The sofa was covered by clothes of various sorts which had been worn into little nest shapes, showing the shape of people's bottoms, presumably clothes weren't put away here. Clare bought some chairs in from another room for us, returning to what was probably her usual seat on the sofa. We sat down and waited for Clare to follow suite.

She did but Connor kept his gaze on the telly. "Hey, Con...,...." Clare elbowed him in the ribs, frowning. I noticed she gave him some frosty eye contact as she spoke.

Connor swore under his breath but kept his gaze on the telly. Clare got up and turned the television off in a huff. Reluctantly Connor turned to face us. Vince introduced us properly and explained the reason for our visit.

Though polite the couple gave each other no eye contact, as if they had just had a row.  They looked at us askew, as if only partly engaged with us.  Clare's tone and body language was a little more compliant, suggesting she was going to find it easier to talk to us than Connor, who sat with his legs wide apart, elbows on his thighs, biting his nails, his face like thunder.

"You are Connor I take it?" Vince asked with stern authority.

"Yeah." The lad groaned, his expression offhand, tense and wound up, as if he was about to challenge us and just waiting for the opportunity.

Clare gave us just momentary, fleeting eye contact from beneath a floppy fringe. "Joe is at friend's haas', 'cos its half term, but I can call and collect him if you want."

"It's you both we need to speak to first." Vince replied, in a formal tone and severe style of language to make it clear he had authority and was in charge here. "I gather you had a Health Visitor here today and she was concerned because you, Connor, had hit Joe. Am I right?"

Connor jumped in with his reply. “Look, I know it weren’t right of me to hit him and it won’t happen again,” he explained in a northern city accent. He blushed bright red, the colour spreading into his scalp, visible beneath his short, spiky hair. He looked directly at us, emphatically, almost imploring us to believe him. "I just lost me rag. It won’t ‘appen again, right?"

"I’m pleased to hear it." I reassured him, my tone compassionate but firm. “Can you tell us exactly what happened?"

Connor took his time answering. He huffed before he spoke but finally started. "We was over there having breakfast," Connor pointed in the direction of the dining room table, "Clare was in the bedroom changing the baby's nappy. Joe was muckin’ about with his food. He took about three mouthfuls then started watching the telly and wouldn't eat no more. I tried to help him but he wouldn't even look at me when I spoke to him, he just kept watching telly, pushin’ the food around his plate and playing with his fork. I asked him to finish his food loadsa times but he wouldn't and ignored me so I turned off the telly. He just wasn’t listening to me like, but that made him shout and scream really loud. I told ‘im to shut up. ” Connor screwed up his face at this point. “Then I couldn't help myself, the noise went straight through me, I screamed at him to shut the fuck up again but he wouldn’t and I hit him on his arm just there.’ (Connor indicated his upper left arm). “I know I shouldn’t ha’ done it. I am really sorry, I just wanted to help Clare. ‘e needs to be given a good bollockin' at times and she won't do it! She's too soft with 'im."

"Thank you for explaining that. We're not here to punish you, we're here to keep Joe and Tom safe." I explained. It was true, we'd get a better working partnership with Connor if he was not hostile to us, he'd listen better and learn better. So calming him down was my aim.

"It is good that you've thought about it and realised what you did was wrong, Connor. But unfortunately that won't be the end of it. We will need to get Joe checked by a doctor and we will need to get him into the police specialist interview suite later, to hear his side of the story." Vince explained in a slightly haughty tone.

I felt he was a bit too stern and expected repercussions in the way of revenge from Connor. I was quickly proved right.

Connor listened to every word Vince said, but I could see the anger building up in his eyes. "Oh, man!! That's crazy!" Connor shouted angrily, his face becoming redder and redder by the moment, his fists clenched up. The words 'love' and 'hate' were tattooed on his knuckles and he thudded his fists up and down on his knees in anger, "It was just a little tap, man! You can't even see a mark there now!"

Clare remained silent, her expression deadpan. She wasn't backing Connor and I was pleased he didn't have her support whatever she said in front of us.

"It's not ridiculous," Vince continued firmly, talking over the last part of Connor's sentence. "Joe is just a young child and much more vulnerable than you. It isn't fair that anyone should have to suffer violence, especially from somebody much bigger than themselves. We need to check out with the doctor that what you say is true. Because hitting a child is not just a bad thing to do, but illegal. You could find yourself prosecuted for assault."

“Don’t make me out to be some kinda bully! That is total shit! I can't believe I'm hearing this!" Connor growled, sitting up straighter, and pointing his finger straight at Vince, as if squaring up for a fight.

Vince faced up to the challenge and spoke calmly but firmly. "If it was an adult you'd hit, or somebody had hit you, you wouldn't be surprised if they involved the police would you? So why should it be any different for a child?"

“It was cos he wouldn’t do what he was told! He wouldn’t eat nuffin’ and just wanned to watch telly. What was I s’posed to do?!” Connor gasped shaking his head, tension and frustration high in his voice. “I’m getting the fuck out of here!” He stood and took a couple of paces towards the door, indignation and fury bursting out of him.

“Hey,” I put my hand out calmly to stop him. I wanted him to stay, so he could learn how he should deal with children, after all, it isn’t easy being a parent or step-parent. He stood for a moment, maybe appreciating the gentle contact. He seemed ready to listen to me. I understood he felt humiliated, as if he’d been told off like a schoolboy in front of his girlfriend. He didn’t seem much older than Joe himself. He might have been wrong hitting a child, but he needed to understand that without being made to feel stupid. Adding to his anger would only put his back up, which wouldn't help anyone long term.

I sought to build bridges between Vince's formal approach and Connor's laid-back 'it doesn't matter' attitude. "I know it seems over the top to go to all this trouble for what might be just one small smack, Connor," I explained, my tone kind, but without missing the point. "The rules, or procedures as we call them, were designed for any type of child abuse, so they have to be used for cases of serious abuse and I admit they can seem a bit hard sometimes when you've got someone who understands their behaviour was a problem, like you do. But the law makers ages ago decided that it was best to have one set of rules to apply to everyone, that way nothing should get overlooked like it has done before, which I'm sure you've read about it in the news. It's the same all over the country, we're not allowed to skip bits of the process 'cos that's how things get missed."

Connor turned away from us. He didn't answer at first but I saw him visibly ease as I spoke, his shoulders relaxed, his grip on the door loosening. "Come back and join us, Connor. It would be good to include you in our plans," I asked with respect.

He dropped his gaze to the floor and nodded slowly in agreement. It warmed me to see how quickly he was talked round, maybe he just had a few things to learn about in life, I thought. He seemed very young and impulsive but open to discussion and change. I liked that. In a way I appreciated his spirit, it just had to be channelled in the right direction and without humiliating him. He returned to his chair.

Even before I trained I had been good at calming people down and I really enjoyed it. That's one reason why I like child protection. It's the challenge of working with people who don't want to work with you that you don't get in many other jobs I like. Funny then, I thought, the only person I can't calm down is myself.

"Can I tell you what I think?" I asked Connor, in a tone almost like reading to a child but not at all intimidating, a tone designed to unwind tense spirits. "I think having a child is probably the hardest thing anyone ever does in their lives, especially the first one or two, when it's all new." I looked around at the group, they were listening to my soft, rhythmic tone as if they'd been mesmerised. I continued, "Making that adjustment to being a parent is hard, especially for you, Connor, as I guess this is your first child. Am I right in thinking that?"

Connor nodded silently, but attentively in reply.

"I think if we can help you by sending someone, a Family Support Worker, as well as me, who can help you adjust and teach you things about running a household and being a parent and managing difficult behaviour that will help you make that transition easier, and we'll have a different, happier family soon. Would that be ok?" I asked.

Connor nodded in agreement.

Taking his answer from his body language I continued in my low, less challenging tone to Connor and Clare now. "We can't avoid the Child Protection rules, I'm afraid, they have to be applied to everyone so no child gets missed out. The police have an interview suite in a house in a nearby estate which is where we'll need to speak to Joe as soon as we can arrange it. It's set up to look like an ordinary house but it has a sitting room converted into an interview room with a two-way mirror and cameras. It's not as scary as it sounds, but that's where we speak to children. It's much nicer than a room in the police station. And we can't avoid having a case conference either. But I'm sure the outcome will be help you find lots of new ways to manage children. It's nothing to be scared of."

"Well, I still ain't happy about this interview or this meetin' thing whatever you called it." Connor frowned with less venom now.

"Conference, it's called. Ok, I hear you." I replied calmly, hoping I wouldn't annoy him so much he would rush off in a huff again. "I can write that in my notes, but I won't be able to stop it happening, they will go ahead with it and you will be invited, even if you don't attend.

## CHAPTER SEVEN

Clare had been silent so far but butted in anxiously. She looked thoughtful, tears were rolling down her cheeks. She looked at Connor with anger, confirming my thoughts that there was tension between the couple. "I'm not too soft wiv' 'im. It's you, you're too hard!" she cried. Then she turned to me, "We'd had such a crap night's sleep, Tom kept us up a lot teething. We just couldn't make him settle!"

"Babies and children are hard work, aren't they? Having sleep interrupted too often does put you on edge, doesn't it?" I suggested sympathetically. "Is Tom difficult to manage too? Did you talk to the Health Visitor about it?"

"Yeah," Connor looked cross. "Joe never listens to his mother. He doesn't listen to a word she says. Health Visitors don't do nuffin' anyway." Connor looked over to Clare as if to check her reaction, she was still crying. He looked saddened and passed her a handful of a loo roll that was close to where he was sitting.

I noticed the little gestures between them. They were touching and made me think they did have a live relationship, even though it was under strain at the moment. "Is this the first time you've hit him before when you don't know what to do with him?" I asked.

"I aint gonna lie," Connor explained, sitting back in his chair with his arms folded in front of him, "It's not something I'm proud of but yeah, a few times. I'll be honest I've only done it when Clare isn't around, 'cos she said to me once that she wouldn't be with anyone who didn't get on with Joe and I wanna be with her. I'll do anything to stay with her, cos I wanna be with her and the boys, it's as simple as that."

"Thank you for being honest with us, Connor. I appreciate that." Vince replied, nodding in approval. "We will need to interview Joe in our specialist interview room though. It's not because we don't believe you, Connor, but we just need to check Joe's story."

"Oh, no, man! There's no way!" Connor growled and ran his fingers through his hair.

"We believe you, Connor. It's just our procedures." I said in soothing tones. "I know I've said it before, but looking after babies and small children isn't easy, there's no denying that. They' are hard work and very frustrating at times."

"Will it be today? This thing about a special interview room?" Clare asked, looking a bit brighter now. It was she who as Joe's parent who would have to give permission for Joe him to be interviewed. I took her questions as approval.

"I'm hoping so, if not, in the next few days," Vince answered.

"Tell us a bit about yourself, Connor, what sort of upbringing did you have? Have you had much to do with children?" I looked straight at him wanting to read his body language as well as his words. He looked straight back at me and didn't hesitate whilst he replied. I took that as a good sign, it confirmed for me that he was probably being honest.

Connor looked over at Clare as if expecting some comment from her. She wiped tears from her eyes. Connor turned away and spoke, his tone sounded frustrated, as if we didn't get what he was saying, "I'm from down south, a few people round here are. We're hoping to get married. And you're right, I don't know much about kids, I never had no brothers or sisters so I'm not used to 'em. But sometimes when Joe's playin' up like, I want to support Clare, so I step in and tell him what's right and what's wrong and he should respect that."

I felt he needed a straightforward answer to the simplistic view he was presenting. "There's a problem with that though, Connor," I pointed out. "If an adult slaps a child or shouts at them, because you're a role model you're also teaching them that shouting or slapping is an acceptable form of behaviour. And it isn't. Also, if you try telling them off before you've got a very good relationship with them they just resent it and it ends up winding them up and making things worse."

Connor listened closely to what I was saying. "S'pose," he agreed.

I broached the subject carefully. "It would be helpful if we could work with you to discuss other ways of correcting Joe when he's naughty, because there are plenty."

"I don't fink there's anything wrong wiv just a quick tap on the arms and it's over!" Connor groaned, but he didn't sound as emphatic as he had earlier in the conversation.

"No. It's not on." Vince said with a touch of frustration in his voice. "You're bigger than Joe, and that makes it unequal. Violence is never a way to solve a problem."

"Let us show you other ways." I soothed. "Having children is the hardest thing anyone can do, I know that, and they do drive you round the twist sometimes. But there are different ways of showing them when they are being naughty that we can talk to you about. It might also help if the baby sees the doctor, or health visitor, just in case there's anything wrong that is making him grumpy."

Connor and Clare both nodded together in reply.

"I could do some work with you both if you like." I explained in an upbeat way, hoping especially to engage especially Connor, who I sensed wasn't entirely keen. "I could help with some of the things you're finding difficult. It might help you Connor, if you and Joe can do some activities together to help you bond better. We've got outreach workers who can work with you to help too."

"Alright then, if you gotta." Connor frowned.

I glanced over at the baby, he was still awake in his chair just looking around. He gave no eye contact to myself or anyone else when they spoke to him. It suggested to me that he spends a lot of time alone, without the stimulation of his parents or others. I had to check it out.

"Do you never get the baby out or talk to him?" I asked Clare and Connor.

"I don't let him out much 'cos he's hard work," Claire explained. "If he's quiet I leave him."

I guessed she meant he was too much trouble to get out. That had to change but I felt I'd been upfront enough for today, so I gave a tactful answer. "I know babies do need some stimulation. I'll have a word with the health visitor and ask her to discuss with you what's best for him."

Clare simply nodded agreement.

"It would be nice to see Joe now, if that's okay. We can introduce ourselves before we meet him in the interview suite," Vince said.

"I'll pop along and get him. He's only a few doors down." Clare left to get him.

Vince chatted with Connor and talked about the local fishing, which Connor seemed to like, and football.

Clare and was back almost straight away with Joe. Joe stood in the doorway, his tiny frame a lot smaller than other children of a similar age. For a few moments he looked at us, the new visitors. He looked like a rabbit caught in spotlights, the tip of one finger in his mouth. He looked not quite tense, but concerned.

"Hello, Joe." I got up and crouched down towards in front of him, speaking directly to him to help put him at his ease. "Shall I tell you who we are?" I asked.

He nodded nervously, hanging onto his mum's hand tightly.

"My name's Louise. I'm a social worker and this over here is Vince, who is a policeman." I pointed in his direction. "He's a special one who doesn't wear uniform. We've come to see if you're alright, then you're going to come and see us in a special house soon, so we can ask you lots of things. It's got all sorts of toys in it. Would you like that?"

Joe looked uncertain for a moment, as if not sure whether to reply or not. He looked up his mum, who nodded reassuringly. I noticed he didn't look at Connor, as if Connor didn't feature on his radar. Then he spoke. "Has it got cars in it?" he asked, eyes wide open. "Cos I like cars."

"Yes," Vince replied turning towards Joe and speaking to him enthusiastically, "And it's got a big garage with lots of parking places."

"Wow!" Joe said with a smile that beamed all over his face.

We explained what time we'd be there and then agreed to meet them later that day.

Job done, Vince and I left. I felt we had done a good job. Neither of us thought Connor was a danger to Clare or the boys, I just thought he doesn't have a clue about rearing children. But he had shown he was willing to learn. And that was a major step in the right direction.

Work continued to be just as busy as it was that first day. There was the usual variety of people needing help that you'd expect in any city social work office, I liked it like that. The variety in such a wonderful setting suited me fine.

Later I went back to the surgery. I walked through the corridor that took me past Gus's room, thinking that if he was in there I would stop and talk to him about Ellie. As I turned the corner I saw him crouched down, talking to a little girl, his back to me. The girl was mesmerised by him, her eyes were as large and bright as a puppy's and a smile stretched right across her face from ear to ear. I couldn't hear what he was saying to her, but the girl laughed and nodded every now and again. Gus looked every bit the perfect family doctor in his Fair Isle top, checked shirt, corduroy trousers and winning way with children.

I waited a respectful distance away not wanting to eavesdrop on their conversation, but I did catch little snippets.

"........so you go home............. take the medicine.............. and you and Teddy come back and see me next week and tell me if the medicine has worked or not." And with that Gus ran his hand over the little girl's hair, said goodbye and stood to talk to the child's mother. The woman looked just as entranced by what he was saying. A few minutes later they said their goodbyes and moved on. Mother and child had been entranced by Gus, and no wonder. He had a super rapport with them. Rumour told me he was single, and would make someone a lovely partner, I thought. But not me. I promised myself I'd stay single at least a couple of years. I think after trauma like mine it takes a couple of years to get confident in relationships again.

I walked up to Gus. "Hello," I said to catch his attention from behind. "I wondered if you'd have a few minutes to talk please?"

He turned round quickly to see me and smiled as recognition washed over his face. "Hello, yes of course. Come into my office."

I followed him in and looked around the room. It looked quite homely for an office. There were some shelves with lots of well- used medical books, there was a colourful mug and coaster, a lunch box, but one wall really caught my eye. It was almost taken over by children's drawings, many of them featuring Gus with ain his Fair Isle jumper, check shirt and corduroy trousers. "Oh!" I said without thinking. "They're gorgeous!"

Gus looked round to see what I was talking about. He saw the pictures, crossed his arms in front of him and smiled as he looked at them, "I've been lucky," he explained. "Young patients have drawn them for me. I'm very proud of them."

"I noticed from you with the young girl just now. It's obvious your young patients like you." I said, was referring to his chat just a minute ago with the mother and daughter. It had been a charming scene, a doctor crouched right down to the child's level, including Teddy in the consultation and then later treasuring their drawings. I'd never seen anything like it before and it touched my heart.

Gus moved piles of paper from a chair next to him. I sat in it as he indicated. He shut the door for confidentiality and sat down himself.

"Have you come about Ellie's Nan?" he asked, looking directly at me with big brown eyes.

My heart jittered inside my chest as I sat face to face with him, but I ignored it. "Yes. I'll go and see her soon," I answered with as much cool as I could muster.

"I've got a wee bit of information," his tone became solemn, "it's not looking good, but it's too early to be sure yet."

"Oh no, poor Ellie, she'll be heartbroken." It shocked me sometimes to think of how cruel life can be.

"Nan has had a series of tests over the last few days. She may have been a bit woozy judging by the medication she's on," Gus explained in his rhythmic Scottish lilt. "There's a few more results to come back, so it's a bit too early to say anything to Ellie yet, but just to let you know."

"Of course." I sighed.

"Aye. It's not a nice thing for anybody, but even worse when there is no family around to help cushion the blow," said Gus.

"And what's more it always seems to happen to the nicest people. I'll have to tell her when all the test results are back, since it looks like there was no-one else," I added. I'd never even met Nan, but the recent pain that had overwhelmed me it made me very aware of how Ellie would feel. My heart ached in sympathy.

"It might help if I was with you when you to give her the news." Gus suggested, "She's bound to have some medical questions I might be able to answer. I'm not going to stop working with Ellie just because she's not what some would call physically ill. I'll work with her as long as she needs me to help her to understand and come to terms with her grief. I'm know it's really busy here and my surgery usually runs over time, but I dunnae mind seeing her in my own time if need be."

"That is so kind," I replied, looking over at him, his whole expression was full of warmth. "She'll appreciate that."

I left at that point and went back to my office. I was touched by Gus's commitment to keep working with Ellie.  GPs are very busy and it's difficult for them to commit their time. But with Gus saying he was happy even if he had to see Ellie in his own time meant I really couldn't ask for more. At least she would have us who she could get to know well to help her with the traumas that she may very soon have to go through.

I went back to my desk with a heavy heart, guessing we'd have to start looking for other parents for her.

## CHAPTER EIGHT

The following Saturday I woke up and opened the front door. The magnificent panorama of the bay spread out before me, the sea glittering in the sunshine, boats busily going up and down the water about their business. The morning sun streamed through the windows and lit up the whole sitting -room. I took a bowl of cereal and mug of tea and went to sit on the bench outside for breakfast in the morning sun.

After enjoying the view for a while, I decided to go for a walk and explore the island. So I went back indoors and got dressed and ready in walking clothes. A path that was heading inland looked enticing, so, shutting the door behind me, I walked in that direction.

The path twisted around after a few miles and led to a low, flat area crisscrossed with fast- running streams. Unusually for this island, there was quite a bit of land in front of me that was just flat grassland. I stood taking in the view around me. At first I thought all was peaceful and quiet, but then I noticed some activity about a quarter of a mile away. There were some tents, a couple of cars and vans and some people moving about. The path stretched out in front of me and passed quite near them. I caught my breath and walked in that direction.

As I got closer I could see more clearly. Two women knelt on the ground busily digging at the soil in front of them and another two people, men I think, standing beside a camping table earnestly looking at something, pointing now and again to different parts of the area. They were all totally engrossed in their tasks.

As I got closer, I could see that one of the men looked very much like Gus. He was wearing a dark blue Aran sweater, green cargo trousers and mud encrusted walking boots and was, talking to a chap also dressed also in outdoor clothes made for bad weather , a scruffy red tartan shirt hanging over the top of jeans and a waterproof jacket. His hair looked as if it hadn't been washed for weeks, he wore a quirky hat and he looked encrusted in mud too.

As I approached I could see that one of them was Gus. I was just going to look away and walk on without interrupting them, but suddenly they seemed to agree on something, nod, and just as they turned away I could see one of them was Gus and he caught sight of me. He waved and walked in my direction, quickening his pace a little and taking big, strides across the lumpy ground until we met.

"Hello there, Louise," he said as he reached me puffed and spoke, his rich accent rolling his words, "Great to see ye. Have ye come to look around?"

"Oh, hi. What do you mean look round?" I was puzzled and tried to sound cool when I spoke to hide the jitters which were going on inside me. "I was just out for a walk, not going to look at anything in particular. It just seemed like something nice to do on a Saturday I suppose." Don't let him know you have time on your hands, he might decide to fill it for you, a little voice inside me said, knowing I needed emotional space at the moment. I took a step back, instinct telling me not to get too close.

"Well, that's a wee bit of good luck for us both then if you've just come across us by chance?" He smiled at me with warmth but stepped no closer, "It' is a really interesting site. Lots of people do pop over to see what we're up to here, especially since we were featured in the local paper."

"Site? What sort of site?" My brow furrowed in confusion. I was a bit surprised by his interest in me and answered with reserve, I wasn't sure of his motives. I hoped he wasn't going to get too close.

"We've not much time till we have to finish here, so we've to hurry and do as much as we can. This is an archaeological site. It was a wee village in ancient times," Gus pointed to a large outline, "But we're just digging this complex of buildings." He pointed to a smaller area. "My brother Callum over there is running it." He nodded in the direction of the other chap in the red shirt as he spoke.

"Oh, I see." Now it made sense. Gus had the piece of paper in his hand that they had been looking at on the table. I could see it was actually a map and what they had been looking at were little bits of pottery and stones, presumably from the site.

"I'll show you round if you'd like." Gus stood aside so I could see all of it. "It's a particularly interesting place."

"Is it?" I asked. It looked just like a muddy field to me.

"Aye, it is. Archaeological sites are difficult to make sense of unless someone shows you the different parts aren't they?" Gus stepped closer to me and stood beside me, his hand gesturing to the whole sweep of the ground before him. I stayed put even though I wanted to walk off. "This is thought to have been one of the earliest settlements in the area," he explained with passion obvious in his voice. "There are quite a few sites like this in these islands, though we're not the biggest, but we are perfectly formed, as Callum says."

"Is it? I've never really thought about ancient settlements much," I answered with reserve, not really happy about encouraging too much personal conversation. But I had always liked archaeology and had planned to find out about it and here was an opportunity right on my doorstep. I followed Gus as he went along little paths through the site, pointing out things here and there and explaining as he walked. We came to a group of stones with some charred black soil in the middle. I wouldn't have noticed but Gus pointed out it used to be a fireplace. He showed me the walls of the building it was in. Once he had explained how it all fitted together I could see what it was, but I did need someone to explain it in the first place.

Gus continued, full of enthusiasm. He didn't seem to be aware of my personal reservations, which was good, since he was interesting. I know I have problems with men, but I didn't want everyone else to be aware of them. Just as long as I kept my distance, I felt I'd be fine.

"Often you get sites of big houses with the traces of little ones inside them, where they have been rebuilt over the years and upgraded, but this one is just a small one." He pointed to the remains of the outside wall. "We suspect its occupants and the villagers moved down the coast for better access to the sea and abandoned this place."

We walked over to the table where Gus pointed out to me some finds that had come from the site, small bits of pottery mostly. Whilst we were there his brother came to introduce himself. As I was soon to find out he's quite an extrovert character.

"Well, hello there. Are ye going to introduce me, Gus?" Callum stopped right in front of us, wiping his hands on an old towel, which was almost as grubby as his hands, and made his effort pointless, a friendly smile on his face, his accent the same as his brother's, "Or shall I do it myself?" "

"Give me time will ye?" Gus replied. He turned to me laughing and rolling his eyes. "He cannae even wait two minutes! Never could."

"I've work to do as ye know," Callum replied in semi-jest., "Ye know as well as I do we've to wrap this site up soon so I can meet the deadline. Anyway, forget the small talk. I'm Callum, this guy's brother and site director. Fancy working here?"

He offered his hand to me, then looked at it, feigning surprise that it was still stained and muddy, "Er, maybe not," he said, screwing up his face in mock disgust and putting it back on his hip. I laughed at this episode, as he'd intended.

"Callum!" Gus answered in a mock angry tone. "She's only just got here. She's even new to the island. Don't be hassling her already!"

“Is she now?” Callum replied to his brother. Then he turned to me, “I know a great way to get to know the island and its people. How about you helping here as a volunteer? We can offer the best workplace scenery in the world,” He indicated with a full sweep of his arm the beautiful landscape around him, “One of the oldest inhabited sites in the Western Isles and the best brownies my wife can make. Oh, but no pay sadly! Or to put it another way, please can you help, we’re desperate!” He laughed.

“I knew this was gonnae happen! Honestly Callum, I did think you’d give my new friend here some time to settle in before talking to her about work! Excuse my brother.” Gus turned towards me with a look of mock exasperation.

“Well I had to get my sales pitch in while she was here didn’t I?” Callum laughed and shrugged his shoulders before turning to ask me directly, “How about it then?”

I laughed at their playful bickering. They were like the grown up version of some of the young boys I see regularly. Should I actually help them? I hadn’t wanted to get involved with anybody or anything in my time here. I didn’t want to make friends. I just wanted peace and quiet and space. It certainly wasn’t what I had planned, but it was interesting and I’d always liked archaeology. Maybe it would do me good to get out and do something completely different.

I didn’t answer for a while, then Callum reached for a biscuit tin from a nearby table and opened it, showing the chocolate brownies inside. He wafted their scent in front of me.

"You can have one, the biggest and best, if you can help us dig that wee area there." He said in a jokey voice designed to tempt me.

He made me laugh. It felt like ages since I'd laughed and I enjoyed the feeling, even though it left me feeling vulnerable. I couldn't say no after that. "All right then just for this afternoon," I agreed.

"Thank you very much for that." Callum looked very pleased then adopted a serious tone, "Your help is much appreciated, I always like to get the most out of a site and this time we're really up against it. It would be great if you could help Gus. That area needs more work."

One of the women called Callum and he walked away from us. Gus spoke once Callum had got out of hearing distance. "I hope you don't mind my brother." Gus looked directly at me, his tone was as if he guessed that I was worried about something and he wanted to reassure me. "He's a good chap and for all our banter we get on great. I hope you would have said no if you had wanted to, don't feel obliged to stay, I'll have a word with him if you do want to go and he will understand."

I turned away from his gaze, putting on a forced smile so he didn't think me rude. "Don't worry. I could've said no if I'd wanted to." Who are you kidding? I thought. I said that with more conviction than I felt. I knew there were many occasions when I should have said no to Simon, when I should have stood up for myself, when I should have said I'd had enough. And I didn't.

“Let’s get you set up then. Come with me, the trowels are over there.”

I followed Gus silently to the boot of Callum’s car where there was all sorts of equipment. After scrabbling around in the back for a minute, Gus passed me a trowel and tray. “There, that’ll get you started. C’mon, I’ll show you where we’ll be.”

We walked silently to the area in which we’d both be working. Gus showed me what needed to be done and how to do it.

“You see the reason Callum wants this area cleared is so that he can mark it all out fully on the plans he’ll draw when we’ve finished. It leaves more complete information for those who may come after us.”

I could see what he meant. The area needing work was a central part of the site and probably quite important to make sense of the place.

“It’s this wall area Callum wants done as far as possible today. I was working here and going along.” Gus pointed with his trowel along the line and explained, “With two of us we’ll probably be able to finish that partPh today.”

“Ok then, shall I start here?” I asked pointing to a place that looked as if it needed uncovering.

“Yes if you like.” He pointed further along the wall, “If I start here we’ll eventually meet somewhere about the middle.”

“Ok then,” I agreed.

He crouched down a few feet away and started clearing the soil in front of him. I watched his slow, steady concentration.

He looked at each part as if thoughtfully deciding where to start and how vigorously to approach it before letting his trowel touch anything. I couldn't help but like him, he was a calm and gentle presence. He was by far the quietest of the two brothers but nonetheless cheerful and warm. I could see why children liked him. He seemed to know I didn't want much conversation and simply dug away at his task. I appreciated that, it made me respect him.

Very soon I was lost in a world of imagination, wondering who were the people who lived here, what were they like, why had they left? They must have had their own stories, their triumphs and tragedies, no less upsetting for them than us.

After a few hours I was aching. I'd been squashed into a cramped position a lot of the time. I stopped and stretched my back to ease its aches and pains. I looked back at my work. The footings of the wall were much clearer now and it was easier to piece together how it fitted in to the different parts of the site. I'd discovered what a lovely pastime archaeology was, I'd been totally absorbed in another world. Dead people were so much easier to deal with than live ones.

Shortly afterwards Callum, announced that it was time to finish for the day. "You see I've worked out that if I don't let people finish with enough time to get to the pub, they don't come back again!" He laughed as he approached us, "Will ye join us?" he asked me directly. "We may not pay but I'll buy you a drink, never let it be said that we don't look after our volunteers."

“Yes. You’re welcome to join us for our post- dig drink,” Gus asked, “One thing you can trust Callum with is to know the best pub for miles around,” he joked.

I enjoyed their merry jesting but going to the pub with them was more than I could handle, “No, I’m going to go home. I will come back and help while the dig is still here, but I’m tired now,” I found myself saying.

Gus stood beside me as I spoke, arms crossed in front of him, just listening. I saw a flash of something, disappointment maybe, at my words. I ignored it, said goodbye and walked off as if I hadn’t noticed. I didn’t want the extra stress that friendships and relationships bought. But I had enjoyed myself enough to agree to come again to help them learn the most out of the site.

I was tired, but happy. I gave them a cheery wave and went on my way back home.

The only way to find out what options Ellie had would be to meet her Nan and get the whole picture from her. So one dull, gloomy day I made the short ferry crossing to the mainland where Nan was in hospital. I did think of taking Ellie who would have loved it, but I wouldn’t have been able to speak to her Nan quite so openly if I had, so I decided I’d do that another day.

It didn’t take long to find the hospital. It was a typical 1970’s building on the outskirts of a small town. I checked at reception which ward I needed, then went along the corridors until I found the right one.

It was mid-morning and the ward looked busy. Everywhere were small groups of nurses with trolleys, some with fresh bedding on, some with coffee and others with medication or equipment to renew dressings. I introduced myself to the Duty Sister who was standing by the Ward Clerk's desk. This is the polite thing to do when one professional visits the client or patient of another. I explained my purpose and asked how Mrs Fisher, to use Nan's surname is, and what was her prospects were for the future.

"It's not good I'm afraid," the sister flicked through some records on the computer and explained solemnly. "She's had an operation to remove one tumour, but tests showed it's not the only one. We're giving her a full programme of chemotherapy and radiotherapy and hoping for the best. But we must warn you that it is an aggressive cancer and we don't hold out much hope. The doctor said we might need to look for a hospice place for her."

"Thank you." I managed to gulp out some sort of reply, I really felt for Ellie. "I'm the social worker for her granddaughter who usually lives with her," I explained and gave her my contact details, "I'll need to support her and her granddaughter whatever happens, because the place she's living now is only temporary. So I'd be grateful if you could keep me up-to-date with her progress."

"Sure." The American nurse took my details. "I'll call you when we know more."

My heart sunk at this news. So Ellie was right, her Nan really could die. My heart went out to her, to them both. But at the same time I knew offering sympathy would only help partly help. What I really needed to do was support her and find someone to take care of her long term if the Sister's prophecy came true.

I walked down the ward to the bed where I was told I'd find Mrs Fisher. As I approached I could see a lady looking much older than I'd expected lying down in bed dozing. For some reason I thought she'd be bigger than she was but the card above her bed confirmed I'd got the right person. She was tiny and as frail as a little bird. Her skin was pale and wan and about four sizes too big for her. Her skin was wrinkled everywhere and wispy grey hair spread about the pillow around her.

"Hello." I bent down beside her and spoke quietly.

Her eyes opened slowly, as if the eyelids themselves were heavy. There were dark shadows under her eyes, she looked tired. She saw me and smiled weakly. It was a smile that was superficial and didn't reach her eyes. Her gaze looked full of worry.

"Hi, my name is Louise. I'm the social worker for your granddaughter Ellie," I explained. "Do you mind if I sit down and have a chat with you?"

"I didnae know she had a social worker." The lady looked at me quizzically.

I realised that probably no-one had told her about Ellie's school outburst. I explained, without making her feel guilty for not being with her. "The school are quite worried about her, that's why they contacted social services."

“Oh, hen that’s a surprise to me,” Mrs Fisher said, her bottom lip trembling with concern.

She pointed to an empty chair which I sat down in. She continued, “I am very worried about Ellie. I didnae know who to speak to, but if that’s your job I’d be pleased tae discuss her with you. Call me Nan, everybody calls me Nan.”

Nan lifted the top of her body to push herself to sit up at the top of the bed, but it was proving a struggle. I walked stood up and slipped my arm under Nan's to help and together we wiggled her to the top. Job done, Nan she gasped and struggled to catch her breath. I stood quietly beside her whilst she coughed and spluttered with a box of tissues close to me, ready to pass her one if necessary. The coughing episode passed shortly.

I hadn’t seen anyone so poorly in a long time. "Is that better?" I asked.

Nan lay back on the bed rest, sighing because of the effort. "Yes dear. That's much better.” She took a few deep, calming breaths before continuing in her lovely local Scottish burr. “Oh dear. I dunnae ken, where shall I start? I am so worried about her."

“You must be,” I agreed, my own anxiety weighing heavy in my voice.

“She is a great worry to me. There is so little I can do whilst I’m laid up in here.” Nan sighed, smoothing the covers under her hands as if to smooth away the problems.

"Could you tell me what other family she has? What about her parents for example?" I was hoping, praying, with everything crossed, that the situation wasn't as bad as Ellie believed.

Nan didn't answer straight away, but remained silent, the agonies of concern showing in her face. "This isn't going tae be easy to say, but you need tae know," Nan she began, her voice weak and uncomfortable as she spoke. "I need tae tell you about Suzy. I am Suzy's mum, I know that, but what I have tae say has to be said. There is no two ways about it. Suzy, is Ellie's mum, and I'm ashamed to say she is a drinker. She never has really looked after her daughter. I've looked after Ellie since she was just out of hospital."

Nan paused, tears welling up in her eyes. I passed her a tissue and squeezed her hand in support. "Go on," I prompted.

"Suzy is my only daughter, my only child. I love her but she's an alcoholic.  Ellie is my only granddaughter. Suzy started drinking when she was a teenager and she kept drinking after Ellie was born so I stepped in to help. At first when Suzy was outtae hospital she came tae me with the baby. At first she would just go intae town with friends and I had the baby just a wee while. Then she was away longer and longer until finally she went tae Glasgow and didnae come back. She used to ring every month or so, she used tae always say she'd come back to look after Ellie. She never did. She doesnae even bother saying it now."

"How sad," I sympathised. But on the other hand, maybe if a woman isn't keen on motherhood maybe it was best if they let someone else do the job. When people do something they really don't want to do they often didn't do it well.

Nan continued without acknowledging my comment. "Once she did come back for a few days. But she kept saying she'd tae go to Glasgow about work. She kept on and on. So I said go, I'll look after the baby. So off she went. She didnae come back. And that's the way it's always been. She comes back now and again for a few days. But quite often she's drunk. I have asked her to stay somewhere else when she's been drinking, I cannae put up with it. Its nae fair on Ellie and I dunnae like it neither."

"I don't blame you. I wouldn't wish alcoholism on my worst enemy." I sympathised, my sympathy genuine, I've seen too many sad and lonely alcoholics to know the impact on the drinker is as bad as on the family. But I had to know more so I asked, "what happened to Ellie's father?"

"We dunnae ken who he was. Suzy would nae say. I expect he was some nae-gooder from down the pub, that's the sort of person she was mixing with at the time. There's never been any contact with him."

"Do you think that has ever worried Ellie?" I asked. Sometimes young people with parents they don't know can miss them. Sometimes they invent a fantasy figure, something they believe about their missing parent to make them nicer. It can cause quite a problem because none of their real parents can ever match up to that. So when they do find their real parent it's a big disappointment. It's usually better for young people to know both their parents from their earliest years even if they only rarely see them because at least it stops them fantasising and they develop a realistic understanding of who they are.

"I dunnae think she misses him at all," Nan explained. "Mind, we've had enough problems wi' Suzy over the years and I think it's put Ellie off parents altogether, at least she's never asked me about him."

"I'm sure you have had enough problems with Suzy." I needed to get round to the subject of the future for Ellie especially, I had to ask, gently, what thought she'd given to her granddaughter's future if the worst happened. I started at an easy point. "Have you any idea when you'll be leaving hospital?"

It didn't take Nan long to reply. I guessed she had been holding on to a lot of tension about it for a long time as she spoke quickly.

"I reckon the only way I'll be leaving here is in a box." She rattled the words out, then fiddled about with a tissue, her hands shaking and tears welling up in her eyes as if she was struggling to continue. "The doctors tell me I should prepare for the worst even if it doesn't happen."

I lay my hands on hers and gave them a gentle squeeze in sympathy, but said nothing to allow her to continue when she was ready.

After a while she looked straight at me as if aware of the impact her words would have and testing to see how I reacted. "I've been very ill for such a long time. Longer time than I've told Ellie. And tae be totally honest I'm tired."

She said nothing for a while, then at last she carried on, "I've had cancer about a year you know. I just didnae tell anyone. There wasnae a lot in the way of treatment they could do anyway. I donae think I will get better. I think it's time to meet my maker. In fact I know it's time to meet 'im up there." She pointed her finger up in emphasis.

"How does that make you feel?" I kept my tone neutral, allowing her to create the mood she wanted.

Nan stayed quiet and thoughtful. I let her take her time. After a few moments she said.

"D'yea want the truth? The absolute honest truth?" Nan cast her gaze straight at me, as if judging whether I was tough enough to hear what she had to say. Then she looked away.

"Yes. I can only help if I know the truth," I said plainly and simply to give her courage to go on.

"I'm ill. I'm weak and I'm tired." A pause again, "If it wasn't for Ellie I'd be quite happy to call it a day. I'm ready to go. She's the only thing I'm worried about."

"That sounds like quite a sad thing to say. Perhaps you're depressed?" I replied.

"I'm no depressed." Nan insisted, "It's just how I feel. I know what the doctor told me, there are no guarantees I will get better. I'm already very old, I had Suzy late in life and I feel old, as if my time is up. I've been in pain many years with arthritis and one thing and another, and over the years it's worn me down. Death is nae to be scared of. It's a comfortable feeling if I can get all my arrangements right.

They are trying here to prepare me for the end, I know that. The doctors told me to get all my finances in order and make a will, that sort of thing."

I sat quietly, listening. Nan turned her gaze towards me at various points in our chat she spoke and I nodded at times to show I was listening. She was quite clear about what was going to happen, and she insisted the doctors agreed. She accepted it as her fate. I felt she was more relaxed with me now that I hadn't laughed at her thoughts or tried to counsel her out of her gloomy mood. I felt she didn't want to be counselled out of what she saw as her fate. I needed to think of Ellie. If Nan was going to die I needed to support Ellie through it and talk with both of them about her future. We needed to be realistic to deal with that.

"Have you spoken to Ellie about this?" I asked gently.

"A bit." Nan gasped and her breathing sounded more difficult and noisy. This was clearly the bit she found most difficult. "Ellie didnae really want to know and just kept saying it'll be alright. I told her last week because I wanted to prepare her and talk to her about living with her mum, but she just wouldnae listen to me when I said I might not get better."

"It must have been very hard for her," I sympathised well aware of how painful those conversations had been for Ellie, "However uncomfortable it is she needs to think about these things. That might have been the day she was so disturbed at school. That's something I can support her with as I get to know her. How about her mother? Does she keep in contact?"

"Huh!" Nan looked away quickly and gave an exasperated sigh, "Suzy? Huh! Look, I rang her tae say how ill I was and ask if she'd come and look after Ellie whilst I was away in hospital. She said she'd be here two weeks ago but we've nae seen hide nor hair of her."

"How did Ellie deal with that?" I asked, puzzled.

"I didnae tell Ellie that part. I suspected as much so never mentioned it to Ellie. Over the years I have watered down what I told Ellie about her mother and sometimes not told her anything at all. I didnae want Ellie to be put against Suzy, because after all she is her mum and Suzy will be around when I'm long away."

"I think that's wise," I agreed. "Ellie could feel rejected otherwise. But if we do need to look for other carers, I can do that and discuss all the options with Ellie and yourself. I'll have to include Suzy too and possibly her father, if we can contact him, since he is her father as well."

Nan turned to look straight towards me and smiled. "Thank you, my dear. You dunnae ken how reassuring it is to hear that. I wish you luck with finding her father, Suzy would never tell us anything about him. I'm sure you'll know how to find foster mothers when the need arises and I imagine they're very nice."

"I'll talk to Suzy about her father. Yes, people who foster or adopt are usually nice. It's such hard work to get approved and the money isn't great so you have to be really committed. It'd be nice to think we can find someone local too." I stated optimistically. I didn't like to say there were so few of them available on the islands, as I'd been told.

"You just concentrate on yourself, on getting better if that's possible. If not, I can talk over everything with you and Ellie and I can help you make whatever plans are needed." I reassured her.

"That's fine, hen." Nan smiled and leaned back in her bed and snuggled down a little. "Now if you donnae mind dear, I'm feeling very sleepy and I really think I should get some rest."

"You carry on." I reassured her putting my hand on hers and squeezing her hands them to reassure her. "I'll pop in again and bring Ellie with me next time."

"I'd like that. Thank you dear." Her eyes gently closed as she spoke.

Whilst Nan herself might be slight and weak, her heart seemed to be as strong as an ox. Here was a woman who had managed to walk the narrow tightrope between her daughter and granddaughter keeping as far as possible goodwill between them both. Nan had instinctively understood that it would be best for Ellie to know her mother in a way that didn't burden Ellie with anger. The world could do with more like her, I thought. I turned to wave as I left the ward, hoping to catch her gaze, but she was already asleep, but now with a much more relaxed expression on her face.

I walked back to the car with a heavy heart. It looked like I'd be helping Ellie deal with one of the most difficult tasks anyone ever had to deal with and that was the death of a parent. It all seemed so cruel, but that's life and it wouldn't help to dwell on the cruelty, the only thing to do was to help her through the hard times and help her choose the best of her options for her future, not that there seemed to be many to choose from.

## CHAPTER NINE

Next day, I walked up to Gus's room at work after surgery when I thought he should be quiet. His door was open and he was working on the computer so engrossed in his task that he didn't notice me standing at the door. I stood and watched him for a moment. He was concentrating intensely on whatever he was doing. I'd seen that look before. Whilst he was dealing with patients he gave them all his concentration, they were his total world, he seemed to want to do his best for them. I liked that about him. I had to knock gently on the door to let him know I was waiting.

He looked up once he heard me. "Oh hello." He answered cheerily and jumped up quickly to clear seat next to him. "Just a wee minute."

I looked at the children's pictures on the wall. I let my eyes focus fully on them and as I did so I could see that a fair few of them were pictures of Gus himself, many of them wearing Fair Isle jumpers, with their bright, zig-zag designs across his chest in an array of bright colours.

"Here you go." He indicated the empty chair.

"Oh how gorgeous!" I enthused.

Gus looked at me then followed my line of vision to the pictures, "Oh them, they're from some of the children I've treated. They're great aren't they?"

“Yes. I thought they might be. The children even got your jumper right in those pictures they’ve drawn of you. They must have really liked you to go to so much trouble.”

Gus smiled and looked down at his jumper, pulling the design away from his chest briefly. “I’ve a lot of these Fair Isle sweaters. They often have some sort of zig-zag design on the front. I guess they’ve become some sort of trademark for me.”

We laughed briefly before changing the tone completely. I caught his gaze as we both knew we must get down to the reason I had come to talk to him. I think we both knew instinctively what it was and that it wouldn’t be good news.

Gus sat in his chair and crossed his arms. A lock of his hair flopped over his brow and gave him a look of schoolboy cuteness.

He looked straight at me, his eyes showing genuine concern. “I guess you’ve been to see Ellie and her Nan. Have you any news?” Gus asked, his expression solemn.

“’fraid so.” I had to take a deep breath before I spoke, the situation was so sad. “I’ve just come back from Nan’s seeing Mrs Fisher, Ellie’s Nan, and I saw Ellie too. Its bad news from both I’m afraid.”

I knew exactly how he felt, my despondent mood matched his.

“I’ve just had the same report from the hospital.” He picked up a piece of paper that looked like a hospital report of some sort and showed it to me briefly. "No hope, I'm afraid. Sometimes life is so unfair."

The smiles we had only a moment ago enjoyed, totally dropped from our faces. Gus looked ahead briefly, his eyes now full of grief. "It's a great shame,"

"It is." I answered, too stunned and upset to say more. My body froze, but somewhere deep in my heart was a little glow of pleasure. Sad though our task was about to become with Ellie I had to admit that I liked Gus more than I wanted to and more than I was prepared to admit to myself, I couldn't help but admire that commitment to his clients, it matched my own thoughts about the job, I felt it was more than just a job.

Gus took a deep breath and sat forward in his chair. "I want to do everything I can to work with Ellie." He turned towards me, care and concern etched on his face. "She'll probably need some counselling, maybe some help understanding the medical facts and I'll work with you on that whenever she needs me. Here is my mobile number." He scribbled it on some paper. "You're more likely to hear about her than me. If there's anything I can help with just ring. Don't worry about weekends and evenings, if there's anything needed, I'll do what I can."

"Thanks," I tucked the number in my pocket. That was an amazing offer. GPs are so busy they really struggle to get through their work. I looked up at the person opposite me full of admiration. This wasn't just a faceless GP desperate to rush through his surgery to get home in time. This person cared. Really cared. Enough to give up his free time. I admired him. "Could you see her with me and we can tell her about her Nan together?" I asked. "She might want to ask medical questions."

"Of course I can. You just let me know when and where and I'll be there," he agreed.

"That's lovely for Ellie, she'll really appreciate that." I looked straight at him, thankful that I was working with him on such a sad case.

"It might take her a while to see that. She'll probably have a lot of anger and issues to work through first."

"I'm sure she will. Certainly as far as parents go she's had a bad deal." I agreed.

"She certainly has." Gus said gently.

The Ferry Inn stood in a very picturesque spot at the mouth of the river that opened into a large flow of water called the Straits of Argyll. Like most places round here there were many boats bobbing about on the waves. I arrived a little bit late to the office party.

"Where have you been?" asked Fi. "I was just about to ring you. I've saved you a seat." She sat at the end closest to the door of a large, long table. I recognised almost everybody in the group, most of them worked at our surgery and some I didn't know I thought were probably their partners. It looked like there were a few people yet to come judging by the empty chairs.

"Sit down." She moved her handbag off the chair next to her. "We've just ordered a couple of pizzas to share between us, there's enough money in the tea kitty to pay so we're giving ourselves a treat."

"Sounds good to me," I chirped, sounding happier than I felt which I was pleased about. I'm not sure Fi was taken in though, judging by the questions she began asking me.

"So how are you settling in then? What is your house like?" she asked pouring her juice into a glass.

"Oh, it's great," I took a sip of the local beer I had bought at the bar. "It's just what I wanted, really pretty with a view to die for, a perfect place to hang out for a while."

"Aye, I thought you'd probably find somewhere nice quite easily. In fact it's quite hard to find anywhere not nice round here. I couldn't wait to get back once I'd been away at university." Fi explained.

"You're very lucky," I replied. "I would have loved to have been bought up round here, I guess you were."

"Ten out of ten there. I'm a local girl through and through. I went to university in Edinburgh but couldn't stand the pace. Now I'm about to be married on the island and I've told my husband to be who works away that if he expects me to move he's got another think coming!" Fi threw her head back and laughed.

She had an infectious giggle and I laughed as I replied, "I don't blame you!"

"I miss him though. He's working away to save up so we have a deposit on a house," Fi explained wistfully. "So how about you? Have you got a partner in tow?"

I blushed at this question but I had expected it. Social workers are generally comfy asking personal questions of new people, after all asking questions is their job. But I felt Fi was only being friendly, I didn't think she was being deliberately nosy, so I did reply. "No. Not now," was all the reply I could muster. I hadn't spoken about it before to people I barely knew and something held me back at first.

"I'm sorry to hear that." She spoke in a hushed, soft way, out of respect for my feelings. I appreciated that. I took a sip of my drink. It felt good to have the attention of someone caring. Then something inside me said what the heck, I felt somehow relieved at sharing my situation so I carried on.

"I guess I'm what they call the classic incomer, running from a bad relationship." I smiled.

"Oh, I'm so sorry!" Fi put her hand to her mouth in shock. "Me and my big mouth! I didn't put two and two together, it didn't occur to me that you could be in that situation!"

"Yup, that's me all right," I smiled, I enjoyed talking to Fi, she was fun but sensitive too. "Been there done that, got the T-shirt." I replied feeling a little relieved.

Fi laughed, "Me too. I've had plenty of useless boyfriends in my time."

"There's some really unpleasant men out there," I replied. There must have been a tinge of sadness in my voice because Fi picked up on it.

Her tone became reassuring. "Ah, but there's some good ones too. You never know you might find one right here on the island, just waiting for you."

I couldn't bear the thought. "No, thanks." I held my hands up in front of me as I replied, palms facing outwards, to show my point. "I had more than enough last time."

The staff arrived with the pizzas and laid them on the table which I was delighted about. Not only was I hungry, but it also helped change the subject. We shared around the various toppings so we had a bit of each. Just as we did so the last of our party arrived, Angus.

"Hooray, at last you're here, Gus," Fi moved the glasses and plates around the table to make room for him and passed him a share of the pizza. He took the only empty seat available, it was next to me.

"Hi," he said as he sat down and put his glass on the table before speaking to the whole group. "Sorry to be so late, I've just been out on a call, I won't talk about work when we're out in public. Suffice it to say it's not been an easy job, I'm on call tonight and might be called out again."

A few heads down the table nodded in agreement, as if they knew what he meant. Not speaking about patients and their private lives in a public setting was a universal no- no, for obvious confidentiality reasons.

For some reason Gus being there made me feel less chatty, more inhibited. But I had to make small talk, since I was sitting next to him. I asked Gus. I had to admit to myself he looked so cute and cuddly in his warm soft tweeds and fair Isles that I didn't dare look directly at him at first. "How's the dig going?" I asked after a while.

"I think it is going fine," Gus tucked in to his pizza. "I spoke to Callum a few days ago and he was very excited because there had been a few finds, a bit more pottery, bigger pieces this time and part of a comb, some personal things, I think. He was very grateful for your help and says he hopes you'll come again if he hasn't put you off too much."

I laughed. Callum had impressed me, for all his jokey ways. He seemed just like his brother, his job wasn't just a way to earn money but something he was really committed to and cared about. It spurred me on to help. "I will, I'd quite like to do some more." I replied, I was happy to help them get the most out of the dig.

"I'll be honest with ye, ye probably have nae chance of saying no. I've known Callum before now call round and get people out of bed he is that determined." Gus's rolling Scottish burr emphasised the half- jokey, half- serious, tone. " You know what he's like. Let's just say that in the nicest possible way he does nae take no for an answer."

"That figures!" I laughed.

"He is determined all right. But only to get a good job done well. I can't really fault him for that," Gus explained loyally.

I had to agree. To say the least Callum was persuasive, but his mission was for the greater good of archaeology so I had to admire him.

There was a moment of awkward silence. I didn't say anything but sipped my drink quietly. I didn't know what else to say. Something about being close to Gus made me keep quiet. Looking back, it was, as if once I started talking to him I'd never stop and I just couldn't let myself do that. So I looked around at Fiona, hoping she would think of something else to say but she was leaning across the table, having a lively conversation with someone in the other direction, so no chance of rescue there.

It was Gus who broke the silence. "So how are ye settling in then?" he took a sip of his drink. Maybe he felt just as awkward speaking to me, I thought. "Are the islands living up to your expectations?"

He turned to look straight at me. I couldn't cope with it and fiddled with my glass. "I'm loving it." I hoped he wasn't going to ask why I left Edinburgh. So I chatted on about anything that came to my mind, to fill a space really. "I've got a really sweet cottage, it's very ancient with a big stone fireplace. I light a fire on chilly nights. It looks over the water and the harbour, it's peaceful and quiet. It's a lovely place to spend a few months."

He might have seen something inside me that I wasn't prepared to admit to myself at that point. "Sounds to me like you're falling in love with the island. This place will get to you so much you'll nae want to leave, I've seen it happen so many times before."

I could feel his gaze on me, whilst he was quizzing me. I rested my chin on my hand, still without looking at him. "Everybody says that to me. But I will have to go back to Edinburgh," I insisted.

He challenged me ever so slightly, while casually cutting some more pizza. "You won't have to go back, there's always jobs round here for good workers."

"I suppose there are. But I was brought up in Edinburgh, my parents were there, all my friends are there. Everything I know is still there. That's where I belong," I insisted. Who are you kidding? I asked myself. Friends in Edinburgh? Most of them were either Simon's friends or had moved on, probably intimidated by Simon's offhand manner, I thought.

"Do you live with your partner or parents then?" he asked.

"My parents? No," I gulped, answering the last part of his question next. "They're long gone. I live alone." I said abruptly. The pain of their loss still stabbed into my heart and I didn't want to dwell on it, especially followed so shortly afterwards by the end of Simon and me. He might have been abusive, but he was solid and reliable. I quickly pushed the thought out of my mind. "But I still have the house they left me. I've a friend, staying there at the moment, Cleo, she's doing a course here for a while. She leaves Edinburgh to go back to America when I finish here, so I'll go straight back to my own house."

He quizzed me while munching on his pizza. "That would be a shame, ye settled in so well and have done some superb work. Not everyone can cope with island social work. You've settled in so well it's as if you were meant to be here."

I hadn't expected that. He'd hit the nail on the head and it took me aback. I had settled in well, I did feel like I was meant to be here. But I didn't want to think I was meant to be here, I told myself I wanted to go home. So I made a joke of his comment. "I expected to be bowled over by the newness of it all, and it has been a great place to clear my head. Pretty soon real life will take over I'm sure. It always does," I said, picking up my glass to drink from, hoping to convince myself.

Gus looked at me puzzled, mulling over my words, but at that moment Gus's phone rang. "Excuse me," he said checking the number. He moved to a quiet space to continue speaking. I could see him switch straight into work mode, business-like, efficient, precise, discussing some prescription details by the sound of it. I was beginning to recognise how he worked now. He was calm, quick to grasp the source of the problem, eager to help. Minutes later he hung up and turned towards us, getting his coat from the back of the chair and drinking draining the last of his drink. "Sorry, folks. I've got to go, duty calls. See you in the morning." He lifted his hand, waved and left us.

## CHAPTER TEN

All social workers have supervision monthly at least, more often when newly qualified. It gives the managers the chance to get to know what their workers are doing and gives the worker the chance to talk things through with someone else without breaking confidentiality. Good supervision helps you get a perspective on your work.

Sometimes you can think you're doing a good job following one plan of action, but then an outsider can see something a different way and sometimes that different idea can help you get work out a better care plan. It's also a good opportunity for social workers to ask if they needed to use expensive resources, like foster caring or nursery care. We're not given much access to the budget. We can ask support staff like youth workers to work with a family alongside us, but anything else we have to ask for so the managers know how much resources are being used.

Janet sat her side of the desk, always the classic professional, notepad and pen ready to jot down notes. I followed her example and took my notepad and pen out too.

"Now, you tell me what you've got on and what's bothering you most." Janet asked. I told her all about Ellie and Nan.

"What a sad situation." Even Janet's usually cool, business-like exterior was rattled. She took a deep breath before speaking, and practical as ever she quickly thought through a plan. "If Nan was to die you might need a Care Order to stop Ellie's mum taking her over. It sounds like Suzy's not up to parenting and Ellie could be at risk if she ever had to look after her."

"I suppose so," I agreed, appreciating the advice. At least if I couldn't stop Nan from dying I could maybe provide a loving, alternative home and some comfort for Ellie.

"From what I'm told you've said there's no chance that she's wanted by her mother for anything more than short visits. But it is something to bear in mind. Unless she has any other relatives she could live with?"

"No. She has no brothers or sisters, nor does Nan. Both of them are all alone in the world, so she told me. As I get to know them I'll ask more to double check, by the time we got to talking about relatives Nan was tired and asked to go to sleep,." I explained. "It's very sad though, even the couple looking after her now will be moving on soon. They move all over Europe working on big building projects."

"How sad! Poor Ellie! Still, I guess she'd need to be adopted or go into foster care then," Janet leaned back in her chair and crossed her arms, a firm decisive look on her face, "But goodness knows where we'd find anyone. You'd better brace her for the fact that we haven't placed anyone older than ten on this island in all the five years I've been here. The only children foster carers or adoptive parents want round here are babies."

"I thought that might be the case." It was the same all over the country. My heart sunk and you could hear it in my voice. I felt totally despondent, I knew what the answer would be to that question, but somehow just having my worries confirmed made me feel really down. Janet seemed to recognise this, she always seemed to be careful about the way her staff managed the feelings they couldn't help but pick up, and she'd help them cope so it didn't impact on their work.

"If her mother agrees we can place her with foster carers, or even adopters if we can find any, without a Care Order. But if mum disagrees we'll need to go to Court. Whatever way, I think Ellie might have to get used to the fact that she'll need to leave the island."

"What a shame." My heart sunk as I heard these words.

"You see that newspaper over there?" Janet pointed towards a local newspaper on the desk. "Fiona and I have just advertised for foster carers in there for a child she's social worker for. This is the third week running and we've still had no replies. Not one single one."

"Och!" I smarted. "It's really hard to tell a child that. Even the teenagers who pretend they don't care do really care, desperately. They just don't want to admit it."

"Even on the 'Be My Parent,' website there are many, many more children than possible parents," Janet explained. "Especially teenagers. The younger the child is the easier they are to place."

"I know. It's so sad." My heart went out to Ellie. I didn't want her going through that, but had to accept it was out of my control. All I could do is write the nicest report on her, as she deserved, and hope that it catches someone's eye.

Janet summed up the problem, "My advice to you is start looking sooner rather than later. You know how long it takes."

"Will do," I agreed.

I met Vince at his office as we'd arranged before we went to interview Joe in the interview suite. I hadn't realised how long it would take to get there from his office and I was early. We had time to kill until we needed to be there so Vince suggested we stop for lunch somewhere on the way. I agreed since I was hungry.

"Phew!" I pulled door of Vince's car closed with relief, "I'm glad Clare and Connor are going to work with us after all." I thought how very differently Vince and I had worked together as opposed to Gus and I. Gus was every bit a people person, whatever he was doing with someone he always seemed to see their point of view, and that helped him work people round to his way of thinking. Vince on the other hand, had an air of superiority about him, as if he was thinking he is the policeman and hence in charge and always right. They were like chalk and cheese in the way that they interviewed people, and I knew who I worked best with.

"I'm please they came round in the end, I was beginning to think I'd have to slap an order on Connor, to make him listen." Vince replied in an offhand manner and put dark glasses on as we pulled away from the police station. "Fancy a nice restaurant?"

Alarm bells rang in me when he spoke. He was so casual about people's lives. I didn't like it. Lunch together can be a way of getting to know each other and I didn't want to get to know Vince any better. Vince's gaze firmly directed on the road ahead of him. I couldn't help but freeze at his words.

"We might just as well go somewhere nice, since we're stopping anyway." He said.

He was right about that. I was starving so I found myself replying, "Ok. You choose, I really don't know the area."

He sat back in his seat, chin held high, in a confident manner. "I know a nice little place not far away." He pushed his glasses nonchalantly onto the bridge of his nose and put his foot down hard.

We got there quickly. The place he chose was a swish, modern place built into what had been an old building. It was too smart for my taste and where there should have been lovely old features there were now smart new things but the food was nice. I thought it was a bit fancy and expensive for an ordinary weekday lunch though, so I wondered why Vince had suggested it.

We spent a pleasant hour chatting over a bowl of soup and found we had had a lot in common.

He was still single, he made that very clear. It was neither here nor there for me, but I thought he made a point of finding out whether I was single or not. You know when people are fishing for answers and they think they're being discreet, but they're not? Well, it was like that. I kept my distance and made it quite clear I wasn't up for dating.

So a short while later we got back into the car and went to the interview suite. It was the first time I'd visited this particular one but it was much the same as any other. Each big town had a similar service for people who've been the victims of personal attacks or children, because it was easier and nicer to give an interview in a relaxed, domestic type of setting. This one, like many others, was an ordinary terraced house in an ordinary street. It looked just the same as all the other houses from outside but inside things were different.

At first you wouldn't notice much difference. There was an ordinary but sparsely equipped kitchen, the sitting room looked just the same too with a sofa and chairs and a huge mirror on one wall. But then looking into the corners of the room you could see cameras and microphones, ready primed to focus on the room's occupants. The big mirror too wasn't as crisp as most mirrors, somehow, the image it made was a little shadowed. But when you left the room you could see from the other side it was actually a window that allowed some people sitting in a room on the side to look in. From the other side of the wall, and you could see straight into the sitting room. The little room was crowded with equipment, screens, monitors and dials to operate the cameras inside. There were no windows in that room, presumably to make it darker and soundproof, to ensure a good recording.

Upstairs was an examination room, so that the doctors could come and see the victim in a peaceful, private, environment which was much nicer than the hurly burly of a busy casualty or a surgery when you've been the victim of a physical crime. Clare and I had taken Joe to see a doctor who specialised in child protection earlier that week so we knew he was safe and didn't need any more treatment. It confirmed what Connor had told me, that he had just hit out at Joe a couple of times in frustration. But would Joe's statement confirm that? We would know soon.

Vince and I arrived at the house a few minutes before the person who was operating the camera arrived and we made the sitting room homely, putting on the fire and arranging the cushions. Vince found some toy cars from the range of available things so we both got them ready, since we already knew that Joe loved cars.

"There." I stood up when I'd finished, hands on hips admiring our efforts.

"That looks very cosy." Vince stood up next to me, looking out over the sitting room. "Hopefully that will help Joe open up to us and we'll get a good statement."

"Yes." I agreed. Shortly afterwards Clare arrived with Joe. We asked Clare to sit in a side room with the cameraman, where she could watch and Joe wouldn't be inhibited, as he might with his mother in the room. I held Joe's hand and led him into the sitting room ready for the interview.

Joe was a bit shy at first as we expected. It took a little while for him to warm up, but we were both used to that so made efforts to help him feel at home. "Look how many cars Vince and I found!" I enthused, showing him our well laid out plan and hoping he'd like it at least enough to play with and maybe change around.

Vince sat on the floor in the middle of a mat that had a whole village marked on it. He'd taken his shoes and jacket off and looked much more relaxed and homely, sweet even.

Joe's eyes lit up with excitement when he saw all the cars laid out before him.

"I've had great fun getting them ready for you." Vince crossed his legs to make way for Joe and patted the floor next to him. "Why don't you come and sit here next to me and we can all play."

Joe didn't need asking twice, he took off his coat with Vince's help, then got down on his knees and moved some of the cars to point in a different direction. He said nothing. I suspected he was shy, and hadn't yet got into his game enough to loose himself and forget about shyness.

"Why are you moving them, Joe?" Vince asked.

"'Cos the road is over there!" Joe pointed a chubby finger in the direction of the edge of the mat.

It's funny how children can see things that should be obvious to everyone. He was right, the road was in the opposite direction. "Are these all the cars that go on there? Look how many there are!" I got down on the floor next to him, playing with children was one of the perks of the job, and it's easier for children to talk openly if there are also occupied doing something else.

I looked at Vince. He'd also noticed how comfortable Joe was now, our gaze met and I could tell by the glint in his eye. It was a signal that we were ready to start the real business of the interview, to find out exactly when Connor had hit him and how often.

"One ... two ... free ... four ..." Joe counted aloud pointed at each as he numbered them. "There are seventeen cars, a tractor, and a police car!" He took the brightest, shiniest his car and made it speed up the High Street, with an accompanying whizzing noise.

"Gosh! That' is really fast!" I exclaimed. I lay down further on the floor resting my head on my hand. Vince did similar and drove a couple of the cars around. Two relaxed interviewers will get more information quicker than two tense interviewers. I reminded Joe of our task. "Do you know what I'm here for?"

"WHEEEE!!!" Joe charged the cars up and down the High Street. "CAN'T RENENBER!!" he replied.

I wondered if you could have too much relaxation, Joe seemed to be totally engrossed with his game and I hoped he wouldn't be too distracted to answer our questions. He didn't look up at me but carried on playing with his toys. That was okay, I expected that, as long as the cars wouldn't stop him talking to us.

Vince asked the first real interview question. I could tell by the look of concentration on his face that he was weighing up his words before speaking them to avoid asking leading questions so they couldn't be described as such questions in any trial, if it ever came to that. "We're here because Connor smacked you, do you remember that?"

Joe nodded freely in agreement.

"Is it something he's done before?" Vince asked, still in very relaxed mode, giving good eye contact, the concentration showing in his expression.

"Yes," Joe answered a little more hesitantly, as if realising that our conversation was getting serious. He was still moving his cars around though.

"Has he done it often?" Vince asked.

"Yes." He answered a little more freely as he pushed another car fast through the village.

"That's not nice is it?"

"No."

"Has he done anything else you don't like?" I asked.

"Yes." Joe answered.

I looked straight at Vince and Vince looked straight back at me, we both seemed to be wondering the same thing. Were we looking at more abuse here? My heart skipped a beat, but I knew I had to continue to be relaxed or risk Joe becoming too tense to talk to us. It wasn't easy, we could have been looking at serious multiple abuse issues here.

Vince moved the cars around a bit so Joe was facing the camera. Joe obligingly moved his cars, unaware of the tactics.

"Tell me what else Connor does you don't like," I asked.

"He hit me, makes me eat all my food and doesn't always let me watch telly even when my favourite programmes are on! Bbbbrrrhhhh!" he sent a car whizzing along the bypass.

Vince caught my gaze this time, our expressions visibly softened as we sighed with relief. It didn't sound as bad as we had thought, but the interview wasn't over yet, we still had to find out more.

"That's not good is it," I explained, "You shouldn't be hit, that is not good."

"No." Replied Joe.

"Tell me about the times Connor has hit you," Vince asked as he pushed a car into a car park.

Joe sat up, and moved his hair out of his eyes before going back to playing. He seemed in no hurry to repeat the stories. He went on to describe three incidents when Connor had hit him. None of them seemed like a violent attack, more just a way to get rid of frustration when Joe wouldn't do what he wanted. Eating was their most common flash point.

"Does anyone else hit you?" I asked.

"No," brrrmm brrrmmm, Joe replied.

"Does anyone else do anything to you you don't like?" I asked.

Screech, brrrmmm, "No." Joe answered.

Vince and I heaved a sigh of relief.

"You know what? I think I've got a good idea. How about if Connor and I talk about different ways to help you do things that you might not want to do without smacking you? Do you think that's a good idea?" I asked.

"No. Yes. Brrrmmmm."

“No, yes?” I asked, emphasising the puzzlement in my voice. “That doesn’t make sense.”

“I still don’t wanna eat dinner sometimes!” he explained, this time making an aeroplane buzz over our heads.

“OK. So how about if I talk about that too?” I swirled around on the floor to give good eye contact.

“Yeeessss.” Connor replied totally engrossed in his game but still thinking about our questions and his answers.

It might have looked like Joe was busy and he wasn't listening to me, but I knew he had heard everything I said and I knew that I had created enough of a bond with him for him to be able to tell me if there was anything he was unhappy about, especially with Connor.

“I think it’s time we were going.”  Vince stood up, I did the same, Joe followed

"And is it alright if I can talk to you again?" I asked to winding up the interview.

"I fink so,” Joe replied.

“And maybe play cars again?" Vince bent down to Joe’s level. “You’re good at that, aren’t you?”

“Yes.” Joe looked around for his mother. I took that as evidence of a good bond between them.

Clare joined us. Joe immediately reached for her hand and held it tight.

“I will want to speak to Connor about hitting Joe, that’s for sure,” Vince explained, “But it doesn’t look like he’s been violent in more extensive ways.”

Clare looked visibly relieved.

I took the chance to plan some preventative work with her. “I'd also like to arrange for our family support worker, Morag Jamieson, to come and work with you to help you with practical things like how to manage the family, especially when times are difficult, without hitting him."

“That’s great,” she replied. It was the first time I’d seen her smile, but she did so and looked a lot more comfortable now. “Connor didn’t mean anything, I’m sure. He’s a good man usually.”

“Okay, we’ll see if they are any better in a few weeks or so. It would be good to build a better bond between Joe and Connor too. That way Joe will listen to him more and Connor will be better able to tailor his punishments to each occasion.”

“That’s a good idea,” Clare smiled as if I’d just given her some really good news, which I suppose I had.

"I’ll pop over and see you next week." I got up and moved towards to open the door for them.

"Bye!" Joe turned round to wave me a cheery goodbye.

“That’s a good job done!” Vince said as he started to put the cars back in their box.

I turned towards him and bent down to help tidy up. “I’m just glad the abuse wasn’t so extensive that we couldn’t leave

Connor in the household. As it is, I think they're a nice young family with a good future in front of them."

"I had the same thought." Vince moved the box, now full with cars, back to its home on the shelf. "I thought Connor's outbursts were just bluster, he's trying to be a parent without any real idea how to do it."

Thank goodness most child protection investigations are like that. It's often that a parent gets over tired or simply doesn't think through how they approach discipline and carries on with an approach that should have died with the Victorians. Usually with a little time, space and the chance to think about things in a non-intimidating environment could lead to people having a whole new approach to parenting.

## CHAPTER ELEVEN

It was a beautiful, bright and sunny Saturday morning. I had the whole day to myself so I made some breakfast, and put my feet up on the sofa to eat it, slowly deciding what I would do. Too much child protection work can leave you tense and wound up so I decided it would be best to do something completely different, and probably something out in the open air too on a day like this. I just wasn't quite sure what when a knock came from the front door.

I opened the door and it was Callum. "Come in," I said, pleased to see him but wondering what this call was about. Callum looked a little solemn, his eyes were just about peeking out from under the brim of his hat and I couldn't quite read the message in them. His expression said he was sad but it didn't add up with the rest of his body language somehow. I wondered what on earth the matter was and took him into the kitchen. "Tea?" I asked.

"No. Dunnae have time for tea, thanks." He lent back on the Aga, looked down at the floor, put his elbow in his other hand and rubbed his finger on his chin deep in thought. Then he continued, "I'll come straight out wi' it. I've got a moral dilemma and I'd like your advice."

I put on my best counselling voice and sat on a chair. In my experience listening to people's problems can take quite a long time. "If I can help I will." But I did wonder why he was choosing to confide in me when he hardly knew me. "I'm all ears," I said.

He left paused a moment before he started. “There’s a person I know whose help I’d really like on my  dig, “ he waved his hand in the general direction of the site without looking up, “But I can’t afford to pay.  Should I go and ask her and pretend it’s something hugely important? Or should I take the caveman approach, go in, pick her up, put her over my shoulder and just take her?”

Only now did a wry smile creep over his face, his gaze peeped out at me from under his hat and his smile turned into a mischievous grin. The penny was just starting to drop for me. “Do you mean me by any chance?” I asked.

“As a matter of fact, I do!” He laughed out loud now.

I had to laugh too, what a mischievous prank! I picked up a tea cloth and chucked it at him! He had me worried for a minute. “Why didn’t you just ask?” I smiled.

He ducked out of the way expertly. “Because asking implies ye’ve a choice! And that’s one thing you’ve nae got!”

I laughed again, defeated but enjoying myself. So much for my plans to be alone with my grief. But I did like being with the archaeology group, it was so different and unusual. And they were so unlike Simon and his family and friends. They had a totally opposite set of values. They weren’t interested in earning big-money, as Simon had been, but helping society understand our ancestors. That knowledge would be available for everybody whether rich or poor, forever. I saw it as a privilege to help. I probably would have gone a second time anyway, even if I hadn’t been ‘forced’ into it.

"Ok!" I smiled and reached for my coat and bag. "I guess I I'd better do as I'm told!"

"It would be much appreciated." Callum stood before me, he'd taken his hat off and was threading his fingers around the brim, and looking straight at me, "But contrary to popular opinion," he laughed, "I will take nae for an answer if you're busy."

"You're all right," I followed him to the front door. "I was wondering what to do today anyway."

"Dunnae worry about lunch," Callum called as he climbed into his car. "I've made arrangements for everyone."

Shutting the door behind me, I looked in at Callum's car. There was somebody I didn't know in the front and Gus was in the back. I'm not sure why I was a bit surprised at seeing him there. I climbed in next to him, the back being the only vacant seat.

"Good to see ye," Gus said nudging away from me on the cramped back seat to make more room. "I dunnae know what Callum said to you to get you to join us today, but I would like it known that I had nothing to do with it!" he joked. "I've been told before about his mischievous tricks! He's well known for the pressure he puts on his helpers!"

Everybody laughed. The mood in the car was very jovial. I was just learning that it was Callum's huge charisma and good nature that made him such a popular chap. Archaeology on its own was interesting and would have drawn volunteers, but Callum made the work exciting and entertaining too. I hadn't intended to be so sociable on the island but I sort of got roped in to help such an interesting project and as a surprise to myself I was really enjoying it. Simon's humour had centred on business people who made mistakes but never admitted it. He loved making money from people, he loved it when any of his rivals looked foolish. He didn't agree with people working for free, unless they were working for him. It made him very dull and serious, with only one goal in life, moneymaking, so this group was a real tonic for me.

Gus turned towards me and said with mock serious tone in his voice, intending for everyone to hear. "Callum has a reputation for spinning strange yarns to get people tae work for him..."

"Don't worry, it's not just you, I've had the same thing," the female voice in the front interrupted. She turned round to speak to me, a glint in her eyes showing me that she was enjoying the company just as much as me. "I'm Michelle, what line did he give you today?"

"It was the 'you have to come I won't take no for an answer' line," I laughed.

"I know that one," Michelle joked, pushing a lock of curly brown hair behind her ears. "Callum has a stock list of persuading tactics when he needs volunteers. I' will have to write a book of them one day. It will be a bestseller I'm sure!"

We all laughed.

"Well I've got to do something haven't I?" Callum waved his hands are in the air for emphasis. "Anyway I'll have you lot know that tonight I'll be buying us all a meal at the local pub, nothing fancy cos I don't have much money, but I won't have refusals!"

"Gosh, this is a first!" Michelle joked. "Are you feeling alright Callum?"

"You'll join us tonight?" Gus turned towards me and asked, his tone gentle as if realising by instinct he needed to treat me gently.

I looked in the distance, scarcely believing what I was about to say. "Yes." I answered simply, smiling. "Well, with Callum around, I wouldn't dare say no!"

"I know what you mean. Best not get on the wrong side of the boss, eh?" Gus replied sitting back and turning towards the front. I'm sure I saw satisfaction in his gaze. It pleased me.

We reached the off-road part of the drive to the dig. "Hold on tight!" Callum called as we bumped our way to the parking place. Minutes later Callum yanked the handbrake on.

"Now, I just need tae check the map to make sure we're digging in the right order," Callum jumped out and laid it out on the bonnet as he directed us to the parts of the dig he wanted digging today. Gus and I were directed to a new part of the site. Gus looked at the plan that Callum held and pointed to the area on the ground.

"Now I think this bit will be quite interesting." Callum moved his finger along the map and looked from the paper to distant parts of the land as he spoke, "I think there might be some features there."

"Features?" Puzzled Angus looked puzzled. "I think it's about time we had some finds."

"Everybody says that," Callum contested, "but there aren't enough finds to go round. Anyway, its features that are the most important, unless you find something really special. Most finds are nae very interesting, and will end up in a box in some museum storeroom. But features get drawn on my special plan, people use them for years in the future for their research in all sorts of different ways." He tapped the plan with a grubby index finger to emphasise the point.

"Okay then." Gus pointed to a small part of the site. "You want us to dig along there, right?"

"I certainly do." Callum nodded and passed us a tray with trowels in. We took them and walked to our spot. We sat on each side of what was probably once a wall, facing each other and gently began to digging the soil away.

For a long time we stayed silent, both absorbed in our task and, as I later had to admit, enjoying his company even though we didn't speak. It was sort of comfortable in the silence, definitely not one of those where you struggle to think of things to say. After a while Gus spoke.

"I expect you'll miss doing this sort of thing when you go back to Edinburgh won't you?" He asked not giving me any eye contact, but continuing to dig.

"What, miss the dig or the island?" I replied, sitting back on my heels. I had been told not to tread on any of the walls all the sides of the dig so they wouldn't collapse. That meant I had to sit in a difficult position, and that got uncomfortable from time to time so I had to shift around a little now and again.

"Either or both," Gus replied as he scraped away at a stubborn stone in front of him, his curly hair flopping about as he moved. He looked quite sweet like that, a bit like a scruffy schoolboy.

I stopped and thought for a minute, allowing the few warm sunrays around to warm my skin and the wind to ruffle my hair. Somehow I felt alive, able to enjoy these little things in life that I hadn't thought of before. I hadn't wanted to enjoy myself here, I had planned it as being somewhere to run away to, a bit like a retreat. But I had to admit I loved it here. More than I expected. I leant down to carry on working and gave a considered answer. "Yes to both."

Gus looked up at me briefly. He looked relived somehow, as if I had said the right thing. "That's good." He said. "You've fitted in very well. Janet is hoping you'll stay."

"Oh, is she now. Why is that? Do they always have trouble attracting staff?" I creased my brow to work out why that could be.

"It's no that," Gus replied. He looked up at me and moved his floppy fringe with a finger away from his eyes so he could look at me better. "You know what Janet is, she's a very canny manager. Once she spots a good social worker, she won't let them go if she can help it."

"Well that's very flattering, but I have to go back. You know that." His attention was focused solely on me, he gave me direct eye contact. I couldn't take it, so I looked back to my work. His gaze seemed to be looking or searching for something I didn't understand.

"Things change. Life changes. Sometimes fate has surprises for us you'd never in a million years dream of, and its best to just go with the flow." he stated quite positively.

"What makes you say that?" I stopped and looked at him, my brow creasing, concerned as to why he was so interested in my private life. Was he overhearing my phone calls or asking others about me?

"You said you came to clear your head." He kept his gaze firmly on me even as I moved about digging. "It's the classic reason and it does make you see things differently sometimes."

"Oh, so I did." I was so absorbed in my work I hadn't remembered, and also he was so easy to talk to that I often said more than I meant to. "I'm not long out of a long-term relationship," I explained.

"Aye." He nodded sagely as if he'd already guessed. "Breaking up is never easy is it?"

"In my case it wasn't the final breaking up that was difficult but the years of torment that came before it." I sat up, moving my hair that had got blown around my face. I found myself talking to him without thinking. Maybe archaeology was like the play therapy that they I used for children, because it was easier to speak when you were occupied. It just didn't feel like I was under a spotlight, and that I was expected to answer. Maybe that made it easier for me to speak. Or maybe Gus just had a way with people – or me.

"Been there done that got the T shirt, as they say." Gus answered as he sat up. His tone told me his broken love affair had been serious, but suggested that he was over it now. He looked from one end to the other of the wall we were working on, his fresh- faced expression almost cherubic. I appreciated his honesty. Simon had never been one to talk about his feelings. I think he felt that was a sign of weakness in anyone.

I don't know why it's one of those strange ideas you get sometimes, but I thought I was the only one who had been treated badly in a relationship. It hadn't occurred to me that Gus might have had a similar experience. So I asked more. "Was it a problem for you too?"

"Aye. At the time. I had known Maureen since childhood but she had more boyfriends than you could ever count. I forgave her many, many times for the ones she didn't give up – and probably still hasn't given up. And then one day I woke up. She'd given me the same old line about working late, I believed her at first. Then I found out otherwise, a friend told me who she'd really been with, and I'd had enough. I knew in that instant that I didn't want to be with her any more. I wanted someone who was special to me, just for me. So we went our separate ways. I was okay about that. But with a brother like Callum, you can imagine, he was really upset for me, wanted to make things better so he kept parading a whole string of single women in front of me, and it made me feel even more hopeless because I just was nae interested." He spoke without flinching, telling me about what was must have been a very upsetting period of his life. He seemed to have peace. I wished I could have peace too.

"Maybe it was just too soon for you?" I asked.

"Probably partly that, but partly because I wanted to be single. With Muriel it was a case of once the penny dropped and I really saw how destructive she could be, I couldn't be with her a moment longer." Gus sat up and clicked his fingers to emphasise his point. "But Callum being a caring big brother just wanted to click his fingers and make everything better for me. You know what he's like. He meant well but life isn't like that. I suppose looking back on it I did need time to grieve. I think Callum just underestimated me, he couldn't cope without someone in his life and I'm not made like that. I'd rather be single than with someone not quite right for me." He paused, "And you?"

"Me and Simon?" I kept my gaze firmly on my work, it wasn't something I liked talking about often, though the time felt right now. "It was pretty similar for us, except we hadn't been together as long as you, about twelve years though."

"It hurts badly at the time, but it seems like ancient history now?" he stated.

"I haven't got to that place yet. I still feel pretty raw and never want to be in that position again." I scratched carefully in the ground, pleased to have something else to think about. As I scratched, something appeared at the point of my trowel. I dug carefully around it, silently containing my excitement until I could be sure of what it was. After a few minutes I pulled out something that was partly round and crusted with dirt. "Hey look what I've got!" I held it up to look at it properly.

Gus came right up close to me to see what I had found. I could sense his heartbeat and feel his warm breath on my cheek.

"Hey," he looked at it closely whilst I was holding it, "I think it's a bead. It looks round."

I teased away the soil, and released the thing some more. Callum, seeing our excitement came up to join us.

I passed it to him gently. He brushed off the soil a little more briskly than I had and held it up to the light to see it more clearly. Gus and I looked towards it. Callum held it in his forefingers and it caught it in a ray of sun. The light emphasised its glorious yellow colour and we could clearly see what looked like a tiny creature inside.

"That's amber all right. With a wee beastie inside too," Callum exclaimed knowledgeably. "And if I'm not mistaken that's a mosquito of some sort. It's evidence that there was trade to and from this part of the land. You dunnae get that round here naturally."

Callum kept it in his hand and took it to the finds table. I felt for the creature inside. Part of me felt preserved too, I had locked myself up too long with a man who wasn't worth it and he'd left me traumatised just like so many of my clients. I felt nervous, afraid, and panic stricken, I promised myself never to get in that position again.

It felt good being out of the cloying relationship, the stranglehold that had kept me in check for so many years. But knowing all the technical terms for what I'd been through didn't stop me feeling totally demoralised. I knew it would take time for me to recover fully. But It felt good being with people, I enjoyed being here with these people. I decided I might even choose to be with them again.

The afternoon sped by, it seemed like just minutes since I found the bead. Pushed apart by the space of a wall Gus and I hadn't spoken much since, though there was a friendly silence between us.

Gus and I found ourselves pushed together later in the pub for the evening. We had followed Callum and his wife Hazel and her sisters into the garden for our evening meal. They kept talking about family things, since one of them had just passed an important exam. I know they didn't mean to be rude but it left Gus and I side-lined a little at the end of the table. I couldn't think of anything else to talk about so I asked Gus about himself.

"I'm pretty boring." Gus sat back and folded his arms in front of him.

"Nobody is boring," I insisted, "that's why I chose the job I do. Everybody is interesting. "

"Well, see what ye think of this. My parents were Mister and Mrs Average, you know 2.4 kids, the .4 being the dog." He took a sip of his beer and turned a little towards me. "They lived away down the valley, except Mum is dead now, she's the one who had cancer." He nodded in the direction of his childhood home. "I was always the good guy, but Callum, as the oldest was the challenge to my parents. My dad was a doctor and I think he hoped we would both follow him into the profession. But Callum wasn't having any of it. He stood out and insisted on studying archaeology and having a string of girlfriends, much to my parent's despair."

I looked over to Callum. He was sitting with Hazel and her sisters. He looked perfectly at home, quirky hat on his head, weatherworn skin testament to years of outdoor working, satisfied expression on his face, laughing and joking with his family. "He looks very settled to me."

"You're seeing him as a changed man now," Gus put his drink purposefully down on the table and kept his gaze on it, only occasionally looking over at me. "He's been with Hazel about ten years and she's transformed him. But I can remember my parents despairing at his playboy antics and casual approach to work at one time."

"Casual? How casual?" I asked, it didn't sound like the man I knew, but then I suppose I didn't know Callum very well.

"He worked on digs all over the world and always came back with a different girlfriend until he met Hazel. I suppose that's the nature of his job, you've got to travel to find work. Our parents thought I'd settle down first as the calm, staid one from the start. Now, it's the other way round. Callum's settled and I'm not."

"Does it matter?" I asked, unsure as to whether or not I wanted to hear the answer.

"So far I've been quite happy on my own." I thought I saw his body freeze momentarily at this point, but I could have been wrong. "I'd rather be on my own than with someone who isn't right for me." He reached for his pint and took a drink. "So that means I've been single quite a lot."

I wondered if his pause to drink showed relief, that he was congratulating himself for talking about something hurtful.

"Do you get pressure from your father to be with someone?" I asked.

"I have done." He nodded, to emphasise his words. "They knew my girlfriend's parents and they engineered lots of contact between us to start with when we were in our teens. We just went along with it. Looking back on it I think it was more my parents plan than anything chosen by us. I just slipped into what was expected of me, thinking without challenging it. I shouldn't have been so surprised when my fiance made it clear after we'd been engaged a couple of years that I wasn't her type."

"That must have been very hurtful." I could feel the wrench of pain along with the freedom that I had felt when being newly single, even though being single was exactly what I wanted.

Gus continued, "It took me a long time to see what she couldn't put into words and then a long time to take her seriously. But she was right. We weren't meant to be together and to try and force a relationship when there shouldn't be one wouldn't work. Anyway, enough about me.

How about you?" He turned towards me and gave me his full attention.

I felt the colour drain out of my face. I should've realised I might be expected to talk about my innermost secrets as well, but somehow I had pushed the thought away. But then it occurred to me I'm always asking people to let me in to their very private thoughts, so why shouldn't I do the same? There was no reason. So I began, slowly, hesitantly, to talk about things I'd never spoken to anybody about, let alone somebody I didn't know very well.

"I suppose my parents were average too, except they've been dead a few years now. I've no brothers or sisters though I have a very good friend Cleo who is just like a sister. Except she' is about was different to me as it's possible to be biologically, she' is big, black and American."

I looked straight at Gus to check his reaction. His gaze was full of warmth, his breathing deep and restful. He said nothing but seemed to be expecting me to continue, so I did.

"My ex was called Simon. I was young when I met him and he was twelve years older. I thought he was wonderful and knew everything. I adored his confidence at first. It was a few years later once I had begun to grow up myself that I began to see that Simon was overbearing, powerful and controlling. He's never happier than when people adore him, he expects, no demands, people to adore him. He was brought up by his mum only. His dad was a wealthy businessman who died young and his mum never remarried because she couldn't find anyone to live up to George. George was adored by his own parents, his mum, aunts and uncles. They always made a big show of him and when George died they simply transferred their adoration to Simon."

I almost seemed to absorb Gus's steady calm presence like light rays soaking into my psyche, and looked straight into his soft, caring gaze. I soaked in the gentle cadence of his voice and breathed in his deep woody aroma. He made me feel grounded and gave the confidence to go on.

"At first I loved the expensive holidays, the silver service everywhere (Simon wouldn't settle for less), the designer clothes, the sleek, expensive cars. Then I started to question his lifestyle and money. He was quite high up in banking and I wasn't convinced the firm he worked for were honourable. The older I grew the more I questioned where he got his money and he couldn't deal with that. To him it simply wasn't necessary to know how the money got there, simply to spend it lavishly and bask in the superior feeling that followed. Then I realised there was no room in Simon's life for anyone with a moral fibre and we had to split, it was inevitable."

Gus turned towards me and looked at me tenderly. "Did you part as friends?"

"No. We didn't just go our separate ways peacefully. Simon was very angry that the little girl that was me, whom he first met and fell in love with, had vanished. He would dictate and demand all the time trying to get the old me back. But once I began to see through him I couldn't put the genie back in the bottle. I couldn't make myself go back to the gullible young woman I'd once been. So after a couple of years of wondering what had happened to me as well as what had happened to him, I insisted we went our separate ways. I think it was probably the first time anyone had ever said no to Simon, and he didn't like it one bit."

I looked round at Gus, he nodded in sympathy. I kept talking without waiting for his verbal reply. It was like lifting a burden.

"He stalked me for years. Everywhere I went he was there, he'd phone me several times a week and insist on sending huge presents for my birthday and Christmas and any other occasion he could think of. He got me a private psychiatrist, telling me I was ill. He rang my friends and told them how I'd mistreated him. Now he has another wife and she's just had a baby. He loathes me according to mutual friends. That's sad since we spent a long time together but I can deal with it. What is harder to deal with is having seen first-hand how humans can change, makes it very hard to trust anyone else."

"I know what you mean," Gus agreed, nodding thoughtfully.

It suddenly struck me, like a shard of ice threading through my spine, that I had just told this chap who I barely knew, things I had never even told my best friend, Cleo. I was lulled into a false sense of security. There was a lot to like about Angus. He was a charming doctor, polite, kind and caring. I loved his homely traditional style of dressing, cords and cosy jumpers. There was no denying he was attractive but I wasn't in the market for a relationship, yet I had just behaved exactly as if I was. I couldn't bear it.

I needed space. I hadn't meant to say so much. I looked down at my watch. It was much later than I thought. "Is that the time?" I said sounding shocked and standing up. The group at the other end of the table were well into their celebration and looked very merry. I wasn't ready for such hilarity. "I must go." I said draining my glass. "I'm expecting a phone call."

"Are you off already?" called Callum. He held his glass up, laughing raucously with the rest of the group about something. Whatever it was they were having great fun. They had drunk a couple of bottles of wine and looked well set to drink some more. "I was just going tae buy you a drink!"

"No, thanks." I muttered, smiling at their tipsy antics. "I'm tired, but I have enjoyed helping you today."

Gus looked concerned. "I'll walk you home," he said finishing his drink and standing up.

"No, I'm fine." I put my glass down on the table and turned to go.

"Go on, let my brother walk you home," called Callum overhearing and laughing and very, very jovial. "He's had a face as long as last week since you said you were leaving the island!"

I'm sure I blushed from my hair to the tip of my toes. I turned and managed a feeble smile with no eye contact then made to go, pushing past Gus to get to the door.

Gus too looked a bit shocked. He rested a finger on my upper arm to stop me. I turned towards him and waited, again giving no eye contact, as he spoke.

"I'm sorry about that." Gus explained with empathy. "My brother just gets a bit beyond himself at times. He didn't mean anything."

I nodded silently and pushed my way through the bustling crowd.

Minutes later I was walking briskly down the path that led towards my house. I turned and looked in the direction of the pub before I went in. I'm sure I could see a shadowy silhouette of a man looking in my direction. Gus. I hurried round the corner on my way.

## CHAPTER TWELVE

A few days later, Ellie and I went to see Nan in hospital. We left on a Saturday afternoon. Even though I don't work on Saturdays, it was a good chance to visit without the hurry of leaving after school and it gave us a long time to spend together. I could take the time off another day, which we call it 'time off in lieu' in our office.

I collected her on Saturday at lunchtime for the four hour round-trip. I always find that young people especially will talk more openly in the car on the way somewhere as long as they're not tired. Ellie was most definitely not tired on the way out. I thought being alone together for so long would give her the opportunity to ask any questions or discuss anything or even just let off steam about Nan's situation. She sat back in the car seat and put her feet up on the dashboard. I let her do it because I thought this young woman had enough to worry about without being nagged about little things.

I think there are two sorts of people when it comes to facing death, there are those who want to know everything that might happen and there are those that just don't want to know until it happens. I wanted to work out which Ellie would be. It was quite a tricky order to work it out without telling her exactly what might happen, but I thought I could talk around that subject anyway and see how I got on.

"So, how's school been recently?" I asked her, deliberately not making eye contact so I could keep my eyes on the road and not pressurise her into speaking.

"All right." Ellie replied in a sullen teenager- type voice.

"Is that all?" I asked in a disappointed tone, "I was looking forward to hearing all about your friends, people who are nice to you, lessons, all that sort of thing."

Ellie smiled. After that she did tell me quite a lot about her friends, the people she liked and didn't like, what lessons she thought the best, what lessons she didn't like. I just asked her open questions, things that she could answer in as much or as little detail that she wanted. That helped a lot and she became quite chatty. Afterwards, I thought that there probably wouldn't be anything I didn't know about in her school. It was a nice feeling to have Ellie confide in me so much. I liked her and sympathised with the angst she must be going through.

“Dr Gus came to see me yesterday.” She said in a matter of fact way.

My heart lit up, I don’t know why, “Did he? What did he want then?”

“Nothing really.” She replied, nonchalantly.

She didn’t say any more on the subject. I thought he had probably just called in to see how she was and left it at that. I didn’t want to get distracted from the more serious and sad subject. I wanted to know what she already knew about Nan’s future and likely death and how much she wanted to know at the moment. It's important to know how much each person wants to know of the truth. Some people want to know everything, some people don't. Both are normal and you need to know which your client is. It would be unfair to tell them too much if they didn't want to know and vice versa.

"Have you spoken to Nan lately?" I asked.

"Yes, she rang last night." That was all she said, it was a contrast to the chatty young person I knew from a few moments ago.

"How was she?" I sensed we were verging on scary emotional territory because of her Ellie's reluctance to talk.

"Ok."

I guessed that there might have been more to it than just one simple word, otherwise Ellie would have been chatting about Nan's day, what she'd had to eat and what her neighbours were like, had Nan been able to have that sort of conversation. But there was nothing of that.

"When I went to see your Nan she looked very tired and poorly." I'd already told her I'd visited, and Nan did look very old and frail, I didn't want Ellie to be shocked so I needed to prepare her as much as I could.

"Yeah." Was the only response I got. Time for a bit more prompting I thought.

"Has she changed a lot in the last few weeks?" I asked, hoping Ellie would answer in more detail.

"A bit!" Ellie lightened up now, she went back to being chatty again when asked to she thought about her Nan. "Nan is great, she cooks great cakes and great meals, she's kind to my friends and if you ever need anyone to talk to, she's there. But she doesn't talk so much now."

"You got a great Nan there." I agreed

"Nan she's the best!" Ellie punched the air in delight.

"How ill do you think she is?" I asked. Wanting to know Ellie's expectations.

Ellie leaned back in the chair looking thoughtful. She started nibbling her fingernails and left quite a long pause before answering. "She'll be all right." Her words had a tone of fear in them, and a note of ending, a sudden stop, as if she didn't want to talk about scary things any more. I sensed her fear and felt maybe it was best to go with that, as long as she knew that she could always come to me or Gus to ask anything if she wanted.

"You do know that you can ask me anything about anything, especially about Nan if you want to. We could ask Dr Gus to come and explain the medical things if you like," I said, turning round and looking at her for emphasis.

"Yeah. I like him." She answered with warmth and interest but still with a definite ending tone to her voice.

"Doctor Gus says he'll speak to us and tell us everything we might want to know about Nan's medical condition because he has her permission. I can sit with you if you want."

"... k," she said in a comfortable, tone if not happy, tone.

We pulled up outside the hospital, Ellie was really keen to get in and walked briskly to the ward, efficiently following all the direction signs and asking the way to Nan's bed. Nan was lying down but turned her head as she heard us approach. She smiled broadly, as if she was really pleased to see us.

“It's lovely to see you.” Her eyes lit up with excitement when she saw Ellie. She tried to sit up to talk to us properly, but struggled with the effort. We came alongside her and went one each side lifting her in her bed, putting the back rest out and plumping up her pillows.

"That's a lot better, thank you hen," she leaned back on the adjusted bed, and puffed a bit with the exertion of being moved. “If I'd known you were coming I'd hae put my lipstick on!”

“I'll do it for you!” Ellie enthused, and began rustling through Nan's make- up bag to find the right one.

"How lovely to see ye, come here darling," she said to Ellie and opened her arms to her giving her a huge hug, "and you dear.” She smiled at me as I pulled out a chair each for Ellie and I.

Ellie put the make-up on her grandmother very carefully as we sat on the chairs beside the bed. Now Ellie was very chatty, and told her Nan all about her friends and who'd said what, and who had done what, over the last few days at school. I wondered if Ellie wasn't chatting non-stop just to avoid talking about anything she'd find difficult. People often do that when they're not ready to hear bad news, it's a way of deflecting reality.

"It sounds like you've had fun at school." Nans head lay back on the pillow. The strain of sitting up and talking was showing in her eyes now alongside the pleasure of seeing Ellie. "I feel like I've almost been there myself!"

Ellie tucked her podgy hand into Nan's. The old lady beamed with pride and squeezed it in return. I was struck by the difference between them. Ellie's hand was pink and healthy, well furnished with muscles and fleshy. Nan's couldn't have been more different, barely just a skeletal framework with skin draped over it. Ellie didn't seem to notice.

"It sounds like Ellie's got a good school, and a good group of friends," I joined in.

"Oh yes, I wouldn't want to change go anywhere else." Ellie laughed. I looked over at Nan as we heard Ellie speak. Nan looked over at me, but the smiles on our faces weakened as if a shadow had just passed over us. Ellie didn't seem to have guessed that she might have to change to go to another school if she had to move in to foster care. But that conversation could wait for another day.

"So, how have you been Nan?" Ellie asked, a little more solemn now. "Have you had to have any more tests?"

"I think so dear. You know what it's like being in hospital, its tests, tests, and more tests." Nan lay back against the pillows looking resigned to her fate but speaking partly with a light heart. "Never a day goes past when I'm not poked and prodded somewhere or another. I don't really know what they're doing, I just let them get on with whatever they need to do."

"Are they looking for something else, some other condition then?" I asked.

"Aye. They know I have cancer, that's for sure." Nan's voice weakened, she cleared her throat and spoke in a more precise, deliberate sort of way, "I don't know what they're still testing for. I like to think that I'm having a full MOT," Nan smiled at her jovial comment.

She stopped and looked at Ellie, who was half smiling, half worried.

Ellie guessed what was coming next, her hands tensed into fists and her face went white, "But you will be all right, Nan, won't you?" A definite tremor formed in her voice and her pallor deepened. She held on to her grandmother's hand as if willing her to hold onto life.

"I don't know, dear, I don't know." Nan took hold of Ellie's hand and held it tightly in both of her own, "I really do hope so. But there's no point in me telling you I'm going to be alright if I'm not, is there?"

"The doctors can do all sorts now, they can cure cancer. I've seen it and heard it on television!" Ellie's voice rose really high and fast now, tears beading up in her eyes.

"Hush, hush," Nan resumed stroking Ellie's hand which she still had in her own. "All I'm saying at the moment, is that the doctor's dunnae ken. Nobody knows for sure how long I'll be around. We will just have to wait until the test results come back."

Ellie didn’t lose the look of anxiety in her expression. I think Nan and Ellie both guessed what the future would be but neither wanted to discuss it head-on.

Nan spoke again, probably unable to cope with her granddaughter’s distress. She spoke in a more cheerful tone this time, squeezing Ellie’s hand for emphasis and completely changing the subject. "But what I can say is that I'm alright today, and I'm very happy to see ye both."

The lighter tone steered us towards a more cheerful conversation. We spoke about the other people in the ward, the nurses and hospital life.  But somehow there was an air of sadness on that visit. I think we all knew what was going to happen in the future. I think Nan knew she was dying and other than leaving Ellie she was quite comfortable about that, as dying people often are.

Once we’d been there about an hour I could see that Nan was tired, her eyelids looked as if they were weighted down and she was struggling to stay awake. I pointed this out too Ellie and we agreed we would leave for the day and come again soon. We left Nan to her rest.

Nan was asleep before we’d even left the ward. We turned to wave just before we turned the last corner, but we could see she was fast asleep. So too was Ellie just minutes later. We’d barely turned out of the hospital car park onto the open road when Ellie was fast asleep and she stayed that way until we reached home.

## CHAPTER THIRTEEN

It would shortly be time for the child protection case conference for Clare and Connor's children and I needed to show my plan to keep the children safe to the conference members since Connor was going to be living in the house with Clare and the boys. I'd spoken to Connor on the phone in with his mother's permission, told him about the interview we had done. He was really relieved that there wouldn't be any criminal proceedings, except maybe only perhaps a talking to from Vince. Fortunately Vince agreed with me that he was basically a decent chap, but a bit young and lacking experience and guidance for the future would be an appropriate way to deal with this situation.

But that didn't let Connor entirely off the hook. He had still hit Joe and had little idea how to manage a child without resorting to smacks to manage bad behaviour. That needed to change.

I called at the house at the appointed time and knocked on the door. Connor promptly came and opened the door for me. "Hi," I said as I followed him into the sitting room, "where' is everyone else?" The sitting room was neater now and Connor had obviously made some effort with his clothes, he was still dressed casually but his brilliant white T-shirt was clean and his jeans smart.

"Clare and the boys are out with her mum," Connor confirmed. I'd asked him if he could be alone so that I could talk to him without interruption about things he might be embarrassed to say in front of Clare and the boys. I wanted to speak to him heart-to-heart so I could really understand what the problem with his behaviour was and help him change. He made coffee for us both and we sat on the sofa.

"So tell me, Connor," I turned so I was looking straight at him. That way I could read his body language best and so he couldn't hide behind mumbled answers. "What was your childhood like? Tell me a little bit about you and your life."

"There's nuffin much to say, just the usual sort of childhood." He shrugged his shoulders and turned on the sofa as well too, to mirror my position. I saw that as a good move, that he was open to talk to me and gave me his whole attention. He continued, "I had a mum and a dad, ordinary house, ordinary school, nuffin special."

"You don't have any brothers or sisters?"

"Nah, I have got one cousin too, but he lives miles away so I didn't often see him."

"You really haven't had much experience with children then."

"Nah." Connor answered honestly, but wrapped his hands around his tea cup tightly, as if he guessed I'd found his weak spot.

"So what brought you here?"

"I got into a bad scene in London, where I was born and brought up like. I had a girlfriend, we'd been going out together about a year, she got pregnant and had an abortion." He looked down into his drink and took a sip slowly and deliberately, as if the pain was still raw. "I didn't want her to have an abortion. I wanted to look after the little one, even if she didn't wanna be with me. I would have the baby on me own like. But she didn't wanna know. She carried on with the abortion anyway."

Connor's tone lowered considerably at this point, he looked solemn. I said nothing, sensing he was gathering the courage to continue. He took a big drink as if that courage was somewhere in the bottom of his cup.

"We split up soon after that. I couldn't face her again. I just couldn't live with it. I thought if she could do that to my babe, I don't wanna be wiv her no more. Who knows, it could all happen again."

"That must have been very hard for you." I know the role of fathers in aborted babies has been researched recently, and they can suffer and feel powerless, if it's something they don't want.

"I had told my parents about it and they thought it was great. They were really looking forward to being grandparents. They were really upset about the abortion too but there was nuffin I could do. As I said, if I could have had the kid alone and bought it up without her, I would."

I sympathised. "It was their grandson or granddaughter too wasn't it? So how did you get to be here?"

"Oh that, yeah. I was at a bit of a loose end one day in the pub, I just had my hours cut in the warehouse where I was working then someone came along that I knew a bit and he said there's work over here building a bridge. I thought I got nothing to lose so here I came."

"When did you meet Clare?"

"I was looking for somewhere to lodge and got a place with someone just further on the terrace here." Connor pointed in the direction, "I got talking to Clare when she was chatting to my landlord. We just got on well like."

"So how long have you been together?"

"About 11 months I sp'ose. Clare got pregnant straight away and this time she didn't want an abortion even though we never planned it. I'm proud of her for that and wanna stick by her."

"Is that why you're together?"

"Nah. S'not the only reason. She's a good lass is Clare. We get on well."

"So what your plans for the future?"

"I wanna to stay here. Its brill round 'ere," Connor waved his arm in a gesture designed to show the whole scope of the land around them. He looked proud and for the first time since I'd arrived held his head high. "I got meself a great family now and wanna stick around. We're gonna get married."

He was relaxed now. I thought I could challenge him. "So how comes you're in this fairytale world you've just described and yet you're hitting a defenceless young boy?"

Connor's gaze fell downwards again and his cheeks went red., "I thought I was doing all right, I just can't get Joe to do what I want. Clare can't always get Joe to do what she wants either. So I thought being firm with him would help."

"So why do you think hitting him is the right solution?" it always puzzled me why people think hitting anybody can solve problems with children.

Connor nodded and looked vague, shrugging his shoulders as he replied. "I suppose cos that's what my parents did to me."

I appreciated his honesty, and felt he needed to understand about discipline in parenting, so I explained. "What you do when you hit a child is you teach it that hitting is okay and perfectly good way to solve a problem, which obviously isn't. It's especially bad when you're the child's role model because they just think it's the right thing to do. As well as that they just get angry and resentful and look for ways to get back at you. It's much better to teach them to be understanding and compassionate to others as I guess that's how you and Clare want him to behave."

"I sup'se," he replied. "When you say it like that it seems completely right. I just never thought about it like that before."

"That's good. The first part of making any changes is realising the things you've done so far aren't always the best. I brought a booklet with me that lists different ways of managing children's behaviour." I found the book and pointed to the text which was written in brightly coloured cartoon style. "We'll go through them with Clare in a minute if that's okay. It's got things like the naughty step, count to 10, withholding treats. But what I also want you to do is to spend some quality time with Joe so you can relate to each other better. What is your relationship like with Joe?"

"We get on okay like, but nuffin special. I don't really think Joe likes me." Connor looked very downcast at that moment, as if he was embarrassed or ashamed that Joe didn't get on with him.

"Well that makes it doubly important to change that it then. It would help if you could take him out alone and spends time with him doing things you both enjoy. Is there anything you can think of that you could do together just for fun?"

"I could take him fishing or summat like that. I used to go fishing a lot and I've got all the gear. There's loads of good places round here."

"That sounds like an excellent idea." I felt very upbeat now, Connor had worked with me well and been very open but I had another plan too. "We have family outreach workers who come into your home every week or so and go through with you different ways of managing children, they help and then come back and see how it's been in practice until you get the hang of it yourself. Would you work with that?"

"Sounds alright." Connor echoed my positive feelings and looked more cheerful now.

As if by plan, Clare and the boys arrived home now. We gave them a few minutes to settle in and for them to find boys something quiet to do. Then Clare joined us for the rest of the interview. We discussed many of the different ways of managing children and arranged for the family support worker to visit before I went home. I left the house in a lighter frame of mind then when I'd arrived. I was pretty confident that Connor's shouting was just a young person's bluster and was something he'd grow out of with a bit of maturity and the help of social workers.

**CHAPTER FOURTEEN**

I arrived at work bright and early the following morning and sat at my desk going through my new emails. For once it looked like a fairly ordinary list of policy changes and updates on the cases I was working on. Mercifully these all looked to be progressing nicely, which showed me that the care plans I had worked out were good ones.

Then Gus walked into my office. He walked over to me and leant his arms on my desk to speak to me. "I've just had a call about a young man who I saw recently and wondered if you'd come tae do a joint visit with me urgently? It's a mental health issue."

"You mean straightaway?" I replied. I'd now seen the expression on his face he now wore many times. It was total compassion and concern and it never ceased to warm my heart.

"Ideally, aye," he replied ticking a box on a form he was carrying. "He's a young lad of 24 who earlier this year was diagnosed with schizophrenia. He's recently refused to have his medication and won't leave his home. His behaviour is becoming increasingly bizarre. He lives in a caravan behind the pony trekking centre where he's been working. If we go in my car I'll give you more details on the journey. It's quite a sad story."

"Sure. I'll get my coat." If the client refused to see us we'd have to consider using one of the sections of The Mental Health Act to forcing him to go to hospital and you need a doctor and a social worker both with extra training to do that. That's why we went out together. Sectioning people was always something to be avoided if possible, because of the sense of defeat patients often spoke of when it had happened to them, and it does restrict some things, like if a person's had any plans to move to Australia. So it was especially to be avoided with young people.

Within minutes we were in Gus's car heading out to the trekking centre.

"So tell me all about him," I asked in the privacy of the car.

"He's a young man called Rob," Gus explained, "he's been in the area about nine months now." Angus changed gear as he spoke. "He moved here from Glasgow and gave me permission to speak to his family and previous GP so I know quite a lot about him. His parents split up years ago and neither of them could cope with him so he was brought up in care."

My heart went out to him, he'd already been through a lot of trauma in his life. "Some people cope with separating parents better than others, don't they?" I spoke with emphasis. I knew from personal experience how problems in relationships can wreck your life.

"They do," Gus replied. "I think the distress led to him being angry and getting in trouble with the police. It was silly things, he dropped a sweet wrapper, a police officer told him to pick it up, he wouldn't and got cheeky. So he got a fine. He didn't pay the fine, so the bailiffs came round. He didn't pay the bailiffs so he went to court and so on. That's how it started."

"Oh, what a shame." I sympathised, I understood how that feeling of uselessness felt. "So it was just really bad management of his life that got him into trouble rather than deliberately causing trouble?" I thought it was a familiar story.

"Yes." Gus moved the car smoothly into another gear. "That's when he started having hallucinations. He began to think he was being chased, persecuted. There could have been some truth in that. He got himself known to local gangs and things and intae a spot of bother with them. He wanted to get away from the city thugs and decided a life on an island would suit him better so he moved up here. His probation officer was really good at keeping in touch with him and getting him the treatment he needed and the job at the local pony trekking centre. He was on regular injections and for a wee while they worked well. But he's been refusing his medication lately. Now he's got his symptoms back. That's what you and I are dealing with today."

"Poor chap," I replied. "So maybe it's just a case of getting him back on track with his medication and then all will be well again."

"That's what I'm hoping. He had a girlfriend here too, she works in the trekking centre and I gather that's off now." Gus was slowing down. I saw a sign saying 'Trekking centre further along the road.' It looked as if we were near our destination.

The optimist in me replied. "You never know, maybe if we can get him better his relationship might be back on again." How comes it was easy to be optimistic about other's lives but never your own? I pondered.

"That would be great, assuming it's a good relationship for him," Gus replied. "He may have been poorly when he came here. People often come here because the peace it gives can help with tough things in their lives. It clears your head somehow, giving peace where there was nae any."

That's what I was looking for too, that legendary sense of peace that you get on the islands. Is it something to do with the hills and the space and the sea? They are all so vast, so enormous, so connected to whatever it is that manages this world, and somehow that makes all your problems so tiny they melt into insignificance. So would it work for me I asked myself?

"So do you think it' was a good idea for him to move out here?" I asked Gus. There was more than one reason for me to ask, I was trying to make sense of what I was feeling in such a peaceful place. Maybe his reply would help me too?

"I think so." Gus answered casually, nodding agreement, "I think a lot of people find peace in the island and settle here."

"Yes." I agreed. The principle seemed sound, I just didn't have any personal experience of it. I changed the subject. "I think schizophrenia is way up there with cancer as one of those diseases I wouldn't wish on my worst enemy."

"I quite agree." Gus turned the wheel as he spoke. "Here we are."

We pulled into the yard of the trekking centre. There were a few people around sweeping and grooming horses that were patiently tied to walls. Angus looked around for instructions as to where to go.

An older chap, skinny as a greyhound with thin grey hair, wearing well-worn riding boots and jodhpurs, waved over to us. His legs were bowed outwards, probably after a lifetime of riding. We waited for him to walk over to us then Angus wound his window down. "Hello there." Gus's accent got richer when he spoke to locals, so I noticed. "I'm the doctor, and this is the social worker come tae see Rob. I think you're expecting us?"

"Och aye, he's over there." The stable manager pointed a wizened, aged finger straight ahead. "He's in a mobile home, over there, you'll see it if you drive along that path. It's the only building there so you cannae get lost. There's no change so far I'm afraid. He was up in the middle of the night trying to paint the stable door. I had to tell him we changed our minds and didn't want to paint it now, I could nae get him to stop any other way. I'm glad you've come right enough."

"We'll do our best." Gus said. "We cannae feedback tell you what we talk about because what we say is confidential but bear in mind we always do our best for people and thank you for calling us."

The old man nodded in agreement. We drove in the direction he had indicated. As we passed a few outlying sheds I noticed one young woman worked apart from the rest of the staff, vigorously brushing the yard. As soon as she saw us she stopped and stood still, and watched us go on our way. She seemed to take quite an interest. I wondered if she might have been Rob's ex-girlfriend.

A couple of hundred yards on we pulled up outside a big mobile home. It looked scruffy and unkempt. Some of the windows had curtains and they were still shut despite its being broad daylight. Some of the windows just had net curtains and these were grey and torn and really needed throwing out. The whole place needed a good clean. Anyone would get depressed living in a place like that.

"This is it." Angus pulled the handbrake on. We got out of the car and knocked on the mobile home's door. There was no reply. We stood and waited patiently for a minute.

"Do you think he'll let us in?" I asked, knowing that some people with mental health problems see the world so differently they can be very wary of visitors.

"I hope so." Gus looked straight at me with a look of puzzlement and concern in his gaze. I knew what he was thinking. He was thinking that about what we'd do if we couldn't see Rob. "If not we'll have to do our best to persuade him," Gus replied. We didn't speak about using the law in case Rob heard us and became too frightened to speak to us.

Angus tapped on the door, a scrap of greyed net curtain moved and I saw a face look out of the window. But as soon as he saw me the curtain shut fast and the occupant was gone.

“That’s Rob,” Angus moved towards the window. “With a bit of luck he might recognise me.” But Rob had moved away too quickly and lost the opportunity.

A few minutes later Rob peered out of the window again, but rather than look reassured he looked more wary. I was shocked at how ill he looked, his skin was grey and sallow, his eyes tired and red, the skin around them shadowed as if he hadn’t slept. He certainly hadn’t shaved for ages as the stubble on his chin looked more than a few days old.

"Hello. Are you Rob? I tapped gently on the window and tried to make eye contact with him. “I'm Louise, one of the social workers here. People are worried about you. They're worried that you might not be very well. We wondered if we could pop in and talk to you?" He went.

Rob appeared briefly back at another of the windows. We couldn't see much of his expression through the frosted glass but you could see he was looking out, and possibly thoughtful, which could be a big step forward.

“I’ll try again.” Gus moved closer to the window. "Rob it's me, the doctor, you came to see me at the surgery, do you remember?"

There was no answer, but Rob was still looking. This time he did see Gus and he just stood watching for a little while. His eyes creased up and looking fearful, but moments later we heard a sound like a stiff bolt was being drawn back across the door, and the door opened just a crack.

"Rob, hello, it's the doctor, Angus, you came to see me recently. Can we come in please?"

"Piss off! Can't you see I'm busy!" Rob kept the door on its chain and shouted, his voice sounding dismissive rather than angry. The door slammed shut and the bolt went back into place and Rob went away.

Gus and I looked at each other, registering the concern in each other's eyes. I moved closer to the window now and Angus stepped back.

Then Rob shouted out. "Go away. I don't need a social worker. I haven't got no kids." Despite the abuse, I thought I detected a note of interest in his voice, or at least less hostility, so I carried on.

"It's not just children we come to see," I answered, calmly explaining our role not for the first time, "We see people of any age if they' are ill. Quite often there are things we can do to help you get better. Will you let us in?"

"I can't. I'm being followed." Rob sounded as if he was engaged with us now, at least he was giving us a reason for not opening the door." In the daytime. It's not safe here. You'd better go too."

"If you let us in we can help with that." Gus replied, we knew that might be part of his illness, the mind playing tricks on him. But if what he was saying was true, we could get the police to help.

Rob was silent for a minute. We hoped he was thoughtful, trying to decide whether to let us in or not. We let him think for a minute. Shortly afterwards we were rewarded with the sound of the bolt being pulled back again. Finally the door pushed wide open and we greeted with Rob warmly. He took no notice but walked in so we followed him until he stopped at a small sitting- room. It was dark with the curtains shut and it smelt musty. The caravan was just as scruffy and dirty inside as outside. We could see as we walked past the kitchen that it was in need of a good clean, there were piles of washing-up on the draining board and dirty saucepans on the hob. The table in the sitting room was laden with full old ashtrays and clothes lay scattered around as if they'd just been taken off and left where they were dropped.

Rob took a seat and we followed his lead and sat on the sofa opposite. It looked like he hadn't dressed properly for a while, he wore an old dressing gown with an old threadbare tee T-shirt underneath, just visible at the neck, and pyjama trousers with well-worn deck shoes on his sockless feet.

“Do you mind if I open a curtain?" Angus asked as we reached the sitting room, “It's just a wee bit dark.”

Rob nodded, in reply then screwed up his eyes at the sudden influx of light.

"Thank you so much for seeing us," I said, hoping to keep up the link that I'd made already, "It's just that people care about you and they're worried about you and we've come to see what we can do to help."

Rob said nothing, he just sat listening, a wary expression on his face. We gave him a moment to speak but he didn't take it, he just sat quietly looking at us emphatically.

Then Angus started speaking. "Do you remember coming to see me in the surgery? About eight weeks ago now?"

Rob's expression creased in concentration, but he said nothing, just screwing up his eyes, looking down and shaking his head to say no in reply.

"You'd been feeling poorly then, do you remember?" Still no comment from Rob, but he was concentrating and listening to every word. Angus continued, "At that time you were telling me that there were people in your life telling you to do things. You'd stopped going out in the daytime because they were there telling you what to do, things like going to muck out the horses at night time?"

Rob's expression screwed up even more intently. "Did I?" he asked.

"Yes." Gus replied. "Are they with ye now?"

"............. Yeah." Rob kept his gaze fixed firmly on the floor.

"What are they telling you to do now?"

Rob's voice sounded weak and frail, he furrowed his brow with irritation, "I dunno, I can't make out what they're saying, I just want them to piss off. It's all the time, day and night, I can't even sleep." He held up as hands and wrapped them around his head as if trying to stop the voices. "They're always here and never give me space! I just want them to bugger off!"

"They will make you tired and poorly, they're very draining. It's not surprising you're feeling unwell. The good news is we can make them go away though," Angus stated with warmth. "Do you remember now when you came to see me in the surgery?"

Rob sat quietly listening and we waited for a reply. Then he mumbled, "…….dunno as I do." He mumbled.

"Well, then you told me someone called Dylan had been telling you to do things that you didn't want to do." Gus reminded him.

Rob appeared to be better engaged now in speaking to us, he was concentrating and putting more thought into his answers. Hesitantly, he started to look up at us as he spoke, perhaps we were helping him relax with us, and pulling him into our world.

"It was things like going out when you didn't want to, buying things like nail varnish that you didn't want or even like," Gus prompted.

Rob just nodded agreement.

"We gave you an injection to stop them intruding on you, and that made all these voices go away. We can do the same thing again now." Gus looked briefly down at his doctor's briefcase. "I have the medication we need here."

"Yeah, I get it." Rob said, pulling his dressing gown tightly around himself. "That was okay. But I don't need it all the time 'cos I got better. That's why I stopped it."

"Then that could be why you are poorly again," I replied. I looked to Gus who nodded in confirmation. "It's the sort of medicine that needs taking regularly I think, isn't that right, Gus?"

Gus explained, "Yes, that is why the hallucinations come back again. If you don't take it you get ill again, but the effects don't show straight away. They only show a little while later when the drug level in your blood has dropped down far enough. You need to take the medicine whether you feel ill or not that day because if you miss too many doses you get ill again."

"Oh. Right." Rob replied. A wary look crept into his expression. He looked uncomfortable.

Gus carried on explaining, probably hoping to reassure him. "It's a bit like taking insulin for diabetes, you need to keep the level up all the time, so the doses are set so you never fall short, if you stop taking it then it takes a while for the effects to show because you'll still have some in your body but in time you will start hearing voices again."

"Now hang on a minute, I feel I'm being pushed into this." Rob sat back in his chair and held out his hands in front of him to emphasise his point. "How do I know you're not just sent from the bad guys to trick me into taking this stuff?"

"Rob, we are medical people, our job is to help people get better. That's all we do." Gus explained with real emphasis. "We just have your best interests at heart."

Rob must've been struck by Gus's integrity, because, after a short pause, whilst he seemed to be weighing up the situation, he spoke.

"Okay then. I'm a firm believer," Rob he pulled up the sleeve of his jumper ready for the injection, "that sometimes you gotta take a few chances in life."

“That’s good, Rob, I’m sure it will help and you won’t regret it.” Angus got out the syringe and liquid and inserted it into Rob's upper arm, then wiped it with an anti-septic pad. "Is there anybody we can get to look in on you, maybe help you tidy the place up?"

Rob looked around him at in the caravan is if he hadn’t seen it for a few days before he answered. "I suppose it is a bit of a mess in here, but I don't wanna cause anybody any trouble."

I could see the problem and had an idea. "We've got some people that work as home care assistants back at the office. This is just the sort of thing they help with,” I explained.” “Could I ask one of them to come and help you clean up?"

"Suppose. If you’re sure they won’t mind," Rob answered.

"I'll do that, Rob." I agreed, pleased that I had been able to do some good. "Perhaps we can come back later in the week?" I looked over to Angus for approval, he nodded consent.

"I’ll ask one of our mental health nurses to pop in too, if that’s all right." Angus clicked his bag shut as he spoke. "We'll come back and see you later in the week, then?"

“All right, then.” Rob looked a little bit anxious, but less so than when we arrived. He held up his hand to wish us farewell. We left the caravan and went back to the surgery.

I knew one thing. Whatever other feelings were littering my life at the moment I knew one thing, that Gus was one a great doctor. He really seemed to have a gift with people, whether old or young. However difficult they were, however bruised and bashed about by life, Gus had both the patience and commitment to stick with them, gently leading them from darkness in to light. I knew that whatever else happened to me, the rest of my life would be all the better because of meeting him.

## CHAPTER FIFTEEN

I hadn't been in the office long the next morning when Gus came in to see me. I was lost in thought working on the computer when he interrupted me.

"Lou," he said, sounding for once gloomy.

Ellie's face came to me and I knew in my heart what he was going to say and a feeling of dread came over me. I said nothing in an attempt to keep my feelings under control but gave him my full attention as my reply.

"It's just that I've heard from the hospital about Ellie's Nan." He paused. "I'm afraid there's no hope for Nan. Her cancer is more extensive than we thought. They can't do anything. It's a matter of keeping her comfortable for what is likely to be her last few weeks."

The back of my throat went dry and I shut my eyes for a second as if to shut out the world. How could the world be so unfair? I screamed inside. Get a grip, girl, I told myself. I and pulled my professional face on. "Poor Ellie," I said. Feeble comment I know, but it was all I could muster. I scratched around for what to think or say. Ellie had to be told, Gus had offered to help, ask him now, I said to myself on autopilot. "Can I take you up on that offer to be with me when I tell her?"

"Of course," Gus answered. "Shall we see her after school tonight?"

"That's fine by me," I answered, keeping my cool, "I'll let Greta know and meet you there."

"See you there." Gus agreed nodded and left the room.

It's not often such a sad task comes up in social work, but there are a few times when there isn't anyone better placed to do the most difficult and of things and we have to be prepared to do it. It's usually accepted that there are people who want to know everything and those that don't and both are fine from a therapeutic point of view.  You wouldn't want to force anyone into knowing what they didn't want to know or withhold information that they might want, so you had to figure out the difference before you started.

I knew we'd have to work that out with Ellie and knew that we'd do that by gently asking her. Gus and I worked so well together that we barely needed to plan out what we were going to say. So it was with a sense of concern for Ellie that I met Gus outside Greta's house later that afternoon. I was so pleased to have him with me. I knew he'd handle it just right.

Gus knocked on the door and Ellie answered it, obviously with no idea of what we were about to say. She was full of happiness when she saw us and she took us into the sitting room, getting us tea while she chattered on about her day at school, her friends, her latest school marks, and her cookery class.

We let her chatter on and enjoyed listening but after a while she seemed to run out of steam.

"Do you mind if we talk about something serious and difficult now?" Gus asked, devoid of expression but full of compassion.

Ellie stopped chattering instantly. Her expression fell as if a shadow passed over her grave. I'm sure she knew in her heart from that minute, if not before. "What?" she asked. I could see her heart pumping fast and colour drain from her face.

"I've had some news today from the hospital about Nan's illness." Gus said in a solemn tone.

"Aaahhh!" Ellie screeched, putting her hands over her ears. She screwed her eyes up tight, as if shutting out real-life., "No! No, no!" She screeched over and over again. "I don't wanna know, I don't wanna know, nooooo!"

I reached over and put my hand on her arm and gently moved it down, "Hey," I soothed, "no one's going to tell you anything you don't wanna hear, okay?"

Gus leaned forward resting his elbows on his knees. "I'm with Lou on this, if you don't want to talk about it, that's fine with me. But I'm here and I'm not going anywhere. If you change your mind just ask."

We all sat quietly. Slowly, Ellie's breathing calmed down and she looked straight ahead, her eyes unseeing. She just sat there, quietly thinking. We all did.

It was Ellie who broke the silence. "She is going to die isn't she?"

Gus just nodded agreement.

"Will it hurt?" She asked. She didn't make eye contact with anyone at that point. I think the news was too great for her, but a tear was making its way down her cheek.

"No," Gus explained calmly and quietly. "She's in the right place. They can give her all the help she needs. "Nobody needs to suffer nowadays."

"Good." Ellie spoke definitely. Tears rolled faster down her cheek, and she wiped them briskly away. Then she announced, "I know where I'm going to live.  Mum will have to tell me where my dad is now, because he's going to have to look after me, isn't he?"

I shivered at the thought. I looked over at Gus and he looked back at me. I could see the look of concern on his face. I felt the same worry in my heart. Her father might not be the saviour Ellie seemed to be imagining. She needed to be more realistic, there might be good reasons why he didn't keep in contact. But how to explain this to Ellie? I had to try. "I shouldn't be too sure. Your mum isn't the sort to be told what to do, is she? Anything could have happened to him by now, but we will find you somewhere nice, don't worry." I reassured her, hoping and praying it would be true.

"Yeah but you two's authority, you're officials really, in your jobs aren't you? I mean, a doctor and a social worker. If you ask mum, she'll have to say, won't she? Then I can find my dad and he can have me, he might even move here and live in my house." She looked from one to the other of us, total confidence in us showing clearly in her expression.

This was just what I had been hoping wouldn't happen. "Maybe," I urged, "Things like this don't always work out how you hope you know. Something will be worked out, I'm sure, but it might not be what you think. Just be prepared for that."

"Not every dad is the right sort of person to be a dad, just as not every mum is born to be a mum," Gus counselled. "Your mum might be right saying she doesn't want to know him. But you're a lovely girl, Ellie, and sometimes these things have nothing to do with the person asking them, the problem is with the other person."

"S'pose." Ellie saddened just a little. "But I can still know who he is and see him can't I?"

"If we can find him. We'll do our best for you, you know that don't you, Ellie and always tell you anything we find out." I reassured her, I knew that she'd have every confidence in Gus and I because we'd always been so open with her and treated her like the young adult she was. She'd appreciated that. I always think it Is better that children and young people are told the truth, even if you simplify it whilst they're younger. That way they can come to terms with reality from the start.

"I've often wondered what my dad would be like." Ellie said questioned, almost as though she was thinking aloud and not speaking to anyone in particular. She sat on the sofa, shoes off, and lifted her knees up to her chin and wrapped her arms round them as if trying to barricade herself from the world. She'd blocked off what we previously told her. "I've often wondered if he has the same colour hair as me, if he's tall or short, kind or rough."

“Hey don’t get your hopes up too much. Quite often people who have been bought up without their parents imagine that their real parents are wonderful and are can be disappointed when they finally meet them.” I explained.

“Yeah, but you don’t know that, do you?” Ellie insisted, a tinge of disappointment in her voice. “I’m nice, you said so yourself, so he must be nice.”

“That is sort of true,” I replied, “He might well be nice inside. But so many things can happen that could have changed that, I wouldn’t want you to get your hopes up and then be disappointed.” I could see the look of sadness in her face. I didn’t want to put her off so much that she would never tell me anything again, but I did want to put the brakes on her fantasies. It was quite a difficult balancing act, especially when you knew, that in the near future she’d be all be alone in the world. Who could blame her for clutching at straws? But if this father man was anything like a decent father, where had he been for the past thirteen years?

We stayed another half hour or so, chatting about everything and nothing, giving Ellie every opportunity to ask anything she wanted but she didn’t broach the subject of her Nan again. Eventually we left Ellie with Greta.

I was at work a few days later when the phone rang. I picked it up. "Hello," I said. The voice on the other end sounded thready and weak, and there were strains of tension and worry in it, I couldn't work out who it was at first, then suddenly I recognised the person.

"It's Nan, calling from the hospital," the voice croaked a little louder.

"Yes, I can tell now, I didn't recognise you at first, Nan. This line isn't very good." I tried to hide my shock, she sounded so weak.

"I... I.... I'm no very well. I cannae talk for long, it makes me too tired." There was a pause which I guessed was Nan gathering her strength. She was gasping for breath and couldn't seem to get the words out so I waited a moment, then suddenly she burst out with, "She's back."

"Who? I'm not sure who you mean?" I asked.

"Suzy."

"Oh my goodness." I said as I remembered who Suzy was. She's Ellie's mum, and she has a major drink problem. That rang alarm bells for me. This was a woman who had already chosen drink over her daughter, now her daughter was about to be homeless, and I didn't want Ellie distressed any more.

As Nan hadn't been to court to get a special guardianship order parental responsibility hadn't been given to someone else, so Suzy would still have legal responsibility for Ellie even though they'd never lived together. Her father would also have parental responsibility even though he hadn't ever seen Ellie.

"So you've heard from her have you?" I asked Nan. I froze as I thought of the possible repercussions.

"She's been here." Nan sounded curt and abrupt. I guessed she had to speak fairly quickly before her voice faded again. "...and I hate to say it, but I'd say she'd been drinking even though it was early afternoon."

"It doesn't sound like she's changed any of her old habits then," I sighed. Part of me still hoped her mother might suddenly become more responsible and care for Ellie, but my hopes were dashed. I reprimanded myself, I had been a social worker long enough to know better and reminded myself not to be so optimistic.

"No." The voice at the other end was getting weaker.

I snapped back into thinking mode. "Do you know what her intentions are towards Ellie? Will she be expecting Ellie to go live with her? Would that put Ellie at risk?" I asked quickly, knowing this conversation couldn't last long.

"Yes. She's going to stay in my house, which I dunnae mind, but she has a male friend with her and she has links at the local pub. I wouldn't be surprised if she spends more time there than at home whether Ellie needs her or not."

"Does Ellie know she's back?"

"No, not yet. And she won't like it either." Nan was struggling to speak, she spoke quickly almost spitting the words out, but occasionally had to stop to catch her breath., "Ellie's been really cross that her mother doesnae even send her a birthday card, ever."

"Where is Ellie now?" My heart was thumping in my chest. Who knows what this woman would do? How could I keep Ellie safe?

"She's is at the neighbours as usual." Nan managed to gasp out

"I'll go and see her," I quickly agreed. "It'd be useful to speak to her about keeping herself safe if her mum doesn't look after her or if Suzy puts her at risk in any way." My heart was thumping hard in my chest at the possible consequences for Ellie.

"I wish you would dear." Nan sounded relieved.

"I'll go straight away." I put the phone down and signed out of the office, leaving details of my whereabouts on the office whiteboard.

The journey to Ellie's place seemed to take ages, but it was late afternoon. Ellie ought to be at home by now, I thought to myself. Luckily enough the lights were on and I could see people inside as I pulled up. I knocked on the door, Ellie opened it and Greta waved to me from the kitchen.

"Great!" Ellie greeted me with warmth. "It's Louise."

"It sure is." I smiled in reply, "I need to talk something over with you."

"Is it something interesting?" Ellie didn't wait for an answer. She went into the kitchen and made me a cup of tea. I followed her and she told me about her day at school. Far from being reluctant to talk as she had been recently, this time she chatted away endlessly which I really liked. But this time I had something I needed to speak to her about before Suzy arrived.

In the end I had to interrupt. I thought I'd better take control of this conversation to get my job done and get Ellie to plan for the inevitable emotional impact her mother's visit would have. "Hey." I said, "I think you better hear what I've come to say. We've got a bit of thinking and planning to do."

That got her attention, she looked puzzled, "What do you mean planning?"

"Your mum's back in town."

Ellie gasped and put a hand to her mouth. Her expression went rigid and pale. "Oh No!" she paused. I thought she was going to cry but she didn't.  "When did she get here? Where she is staying? Will she want me back? 'Cos I'm not going with her!" she said. Tears welled up in her eyes.

"I don't know the answer to all of those questions yet," I explained, trying to keep myself calm as well as Ellie. "I just had a phone call from Nan who'd had a visit from Suzy. She was worried that Suzy would want you to come and stay in her place in Glasgow."

"No! No! No! No! I can't do that!" Ellie's face twisted in despair. "She'll get drunk, I know it!'

"Hey." I put my hands on her forearms and held her tightly to calm her down. "You don't have to go with her you know. You can just say no and ring me if you want. If your mum insists you go we can get an Emergency Protection Order from the police so that will give social services more power than your mother to say where you stay and not your mum."

Ellie still looked distressed and puzzled. I asked her why.

"Wouldn't you be happy about saying no?" I thought she'd be pleased at that, and was puzzled that she didn't seem to be.

"She's my mum. I'm supposed to love her! Part of me says I should be with her, but I know I can't!" Ellie cried. I could understand how she could feel she should be loyal to her mum and not want to challenge her. I thought if she wanted to hang onto whatever shreds of a relationship she had with her mother, then she must be allowed to do that. After all, it was likely that she would be her only blood relation soon.

"Hey, calm down," I said, putting my arm around her shoulder. I grabbed a handful of tissues and passed I them to her to her to dry her eyes. Sometimes actions speak louder than words and I needed every scrap of Ellie's concentration to listen to me. So I turned to face her so I could see her properly and talk to her directly. I needed some way of ensuring that, whatever happened, if or when her mother turned up, Ellie would be safe.

"Look, I know we have no court order that I can use to stop you going to stay with her if she turns up and demands that you go with her. But if she's just expecting you to go along to Nan's house which is just further along the terrace, you could come back here if things get bad. Would that be okay? Sometimes birth parents aren't the right people to bring up children. Every social worker will tell you of times when a child is best bought up by people than the natural parents. It's no crime, it's just how things are," I explained.

Ellie's sobbing got easier now, and I could see she was listening. "S'pose so," she replied reaching for a tissue and wiping her eyes.

"I'll ask Greta if you could have a key so you can come back any time you need to." I called to Greta explaining what we wanted with some actions and getting her permission. Greta gave her a key.

"There, now that's one plan isn't?" I looked straight at Ellie, she nodded in reply. "We're going to have another. You've got a mobile haven't you? You ring me anytime you get scared, I'll give you my mobile number and ring if you're at all worried." There isn't a rule that you shouldn't give your personal number out, it was at our discretion and I knew that Ellie would respect that and I was too worried about her not to do it. She had become very special to me and I wanted to do my best for her.

We tapped the numbers into our phones, ringing them to check that they worked.

"Now we've got plans to keep you safe. I'm going to go now, okay," I tucked my phone into my bag. "You will be okay, and in one way if mum does try to make you go with her, then we have evidence to use against her if we need it in court."

Ellie used her sleeve to give her eyes one final wipe as she spoke, "I suppose so."

I left feeling that even if we couldn't stop Suzy demanding that Ellie go with her, at least we could keep her safe. Sometimes people have to do act to make things clear in our minds and this seemed to be just like that. If it had been some time since Ellie had seen her mum it was quite understandable that Ellie wouldn't want to upset her mum straight away, it was good to see her so loyal.

I couldn't help worrying about Ellie though. You don't just switch off with this job. You're dealing with real people and real lives. I had a nasty shock on the way home, as I turned a corner, straight ahead of me in the road coming towards me, much too fast and on the wrong side, was an ancient, battered old saloon car.

As soon as I saw it I hit the car horn as hard as I could and swerved out of the way. Fortunately, just in the nick of time the other car swerved too and we missed each other by a fraction of an inch. I was still shaking when I got home. It took a long, deep, warm bath with a cup of tea to calm me down.

I didn't know it then, I didn't have enough time to see the driver of the other car, but if I had I'd have seen that the driver had the same colour hair as Ellie, the same colour eyes and that the little dimples in Ellie's cheeks were just the same as the driver's. She was none other than Suzy, Ellie's mother with her partner Paul.

**CHAPTER SIXTEEN**

I got into to the office a little late the next day. There were piles of messages for the duty social worker and a few messages from Ellie who hadn't wanted to bother me on my mobile. I guess she was anxious about her mother so I rang her back promptly. She picked up quickly and sounded relieved to hear me.

"How did it go yesterday, did your mum turn up?" I asked, concerned that her mother might have caused trouble for Ellie.

"Yes, she did." Ellie sounded in control, at least at first. "Mum's not been too bad. She's staying in Nan's house with her boyfriend, Paul. Mum's quite happy for me to stay in this house with Greta, 'cos that's what I said I'd rather do. I don't think they want me to stay with them anyway cos then they'd have to go shopping for food for me. "

"It's good to hear that she's giving you a choice," I said, breathing a sigh of relief. "You were worried that she'd want you to stay with her, weren't you?"

"Yeah, it's been okay-ish." Ellie emphasised the word ish. It alerted me to the fact that she was becoming more tense and shaky, as if she was trying to hold in her anxiety and only just about managing it. "She stinks of drink all the time, and Paul too."

"Yuck." I tut-tutted. "Do I take it you still don't want to live with your mum?" I wanted to know if actually meeting her mum in the flesh when Nan wasn't around had changed Ellie's opinion of her. Sometimes you imagine something's going to be very bad, but when it happens it isn't.

"No way!" Ellie stated firmly with disgust, as teenagers do. "I don't trust her to be there when I need her and even if she is there in her body she is usually drunk. And anyway if she's not drunk she's usually singing with her band, Sounds like Suzy. She isn't even in till long past midnight and never gets up till late."

"I see what you mean. Well then, we'll see what your mum offers because we have to look at her ideas first, even if we disagree with them."

"I don't think she'll know anywhere anyway. Where else could I live when Nan does die? Where else can I go if I don't go to mum's? And we don't even know about Dad yet," Ellie asked. I could tell by the tremor in her voice that she was close to tears. I had to admit I felt the same myself. Ellie was such a lovely young girl, how could life treat her so badly? It didn't seem right. I didn't envy her, she was looking at a choice between a drunken mum and who knows what?

"Even if it's just a formality I have to ask your mum," I tried to keep the worry out of my voice as I spoke, Ellie needed to have confidence that I could solve this problem with her. "Then we'll need to look for either a foster home, or even better someone who could adopt you."

"What's the difference?" Ellie swallowed back a sob as she answered.

I guessed she had no idea that care of whatever sort, either fostering, adoption or even a care home, might be miles away, not even on the island. That would mean in such a short life she had lost a mother, and a loving grandma, all her school friends and everything she'd ever known and loved. Life was so unfair and Ellie's pain twisted my heart.

I gulped back a sob and stopped myself dwelling on the worst. "Fostering is a bit like what you have now with Greta, you're happy there and can stay there but it might not be forever. Adoption is just like you were born to that family, you belong there. Adoptive parents are your legal parents once the final adoption order is made."

"Oh I get it. So adoption's best then?" she sounded a little bit more light-hearted at this point.

"Yes, but don't rule out fostering," I agreed. I don't suppose she'd ever thought of how hard it is to get any alternative family for an older child whatever the legal status. I couldn't bear to tell her that often teenage children struggle to get any sort of a home. So many people want babies. Teenagers often end up in residential units or with short-term foster carers.

I changed the subject. There was no need to dwell on the future now. Gus had said Nan would at least have had a few more weeks. "Yes. Anyway, this isn't the sort of conversation we should have on the phone. Do you know if your mum would be in if I called round to see her later this afternoon?"

"Probably." Ellie replied, a deep intake of breath told me she was taking control of herself now. "I'm going with mum to see Nan later, but we could go after you've been."

"That would suit me fine."

"I'll pop along and tell her, shall I? I think she's in because the car is there."

"Okay," I agreed, "I'll need to see them alone for a while though."

"That's all right. See you later." Ellie put the phone down.

Almost all the time I'd prefer everyone to be in the room when I'm talking about them, but this was one of those times I didn't think it was suitable for Ellie to be in the room with us when discussing her. I needed to ask Suzy what plans she had for where Ellie was to live if or when Nan did died. And that could be a difficult conversation, especially if Suzy said that she would take her back to her house with her new boyfriend. I'd need to know if he was a safe person to have such close contact with such a vulnerable person as Ellie and if their home in general was suitable for a child and I can't see either conversation going down well. After all, Suzy had given Ellie up once, we didn't want it happening again. It probably was the case that Suzy didn't want Ellie to live with her anymore, but I had to give Suzy the opportunity to explain herself in private. I carried on with the duty work until it was time to go and meet the family.

As usual, more jobs come along than I wanted so I ended up dashing to see Ellie. I pulled up in my usual spot and noticed a different car in the car park. I recognised it from my near miss yesterday. It was bashed about quite a lot and had seen better days judging by the look of it. I guessed it belonged to Suzy and her boyfriend which backed up everything I'd heard about Suzy so far.

I walked up to Nan's house where Ellie had said she'd be waiting for me, she saw me walking along the path and jumped up to let me in.

"Hello," she led me into the front sitting room. "It's Louise, my social worker!" She shouted inside by way of introduction.

Suzy and Paul were sitting on the sofa waiting for me. Suzy didn't see, very tall with long brown hair in a thin ponytail down her back. She wore a black tracksuit and trainers. Paul wasn't much taller, he wore some old jeans and a black T-shirt with a motif of a heavy metal band on the front. Both of them had piercings, not just in their ears, Suzy had one in her nose and lip. I counted three holes in Paul's ears and six in Suzy's with a variety of different rings in them. Suzy had lots of rings on her fingers and Paul had Peace and Love tattooed on his knuckles and big thick rings beneath them. Paul looked quite chunky, with a belly tumbling over his belt. Susie looked quite thin, as if she often missed meals. Despite their different colouring, their skin was tinged with pale grey, and they both smelt of drink.

The air was thick with the smell of cigarette smoke and I screwed up my eyes until they adjusted to it. I greeted the couple and went to the sofa to shake Suzy and Paul's hands before sitting down in a chair opposite them. They grumbled a 'hello'.

"Thank you for introducing me," I said to Ellie and balancing my notebook on my lap. "Do you mind if I speak to them alone now?"

"Aw, are you sure I can't stay?" Ellie tilted her head and looked at me with pleading eyes that were just like a puppy's, "I won't interrupt, and you are going to be talking about me after all."

"You do as the lady says," Suzy growled firmly, her voice roughened by years of smoking.

"Not this time Ellie." I smiled at her. I couldn't help admiring her cheeky questioning.

"Okay then, I just thought I'd try." Ellie shrugged her shoulders and walked out.

I waited a few minutes till I heard the front door click behind her before I spoke.

I began quite formally, "Right then, nice to meet you and can I thank you for staying in to see me."

Paul and Suzy said nothing, the smoke from their cigarettes wafting through the room around me. Suzy just sat, her expression giving away nothing away, but her jaw tightening defensively.

I was interested to see how she would react when we got further into the interview especially when we got onto emotional stuff, there was not the slightest speck emotion from her, even though her mother was shortly to die leaving her daughter homeless. Was this woman really made of stone or was it just an act that she'd drop when the time was right for her? I continued, “What I wanted to see you about was Ellie, obviously, and where she’s staying both now and in the future.”

The couple still said nothing, just listened. I continued slightly phased by the lack of communication.

“Firstly, I must let you know though that even though you know Greta and her husband, any child who stays with someone not of their family must be vetted by us.” I flicked through the pile of papers I had on my lap.

“What for?” Paul screwed up his face and queried.

“It’s what the government call Private Fostering. They are rules that exist for any people caring for a child who is not their own or part of their close biological family. The parent’s and carers are obliged to inform us when a stay exceeds twenty eight days, or earlier if they know the stay will be longer than that from the outset. The checks cover not just police checks but every aspect of life, just to make sure that the child is safe in their care. It does mean that Greta and Pieter will need to be checked and vetted by us.”

"More than twenty-eight days have passed since she’s been there I think? Are we in any trouble because we haven't done that yet?" Paul asked.

I nodded in reply. “No-one is in any trouble, because no-one knew at first how long it would be for, it was only supposed to be a few days. I have started the process now, and one of the requirements is to speak to the child’s natural parents and of course I’m doing that now.”

They shook their heads in agreement. “I have started police checks, which is the most important thing. And another social worker will do the vetting to avoid a conflict of interest.”

“Do you think it’ll cause any problems?” Paul seemed more interested than Suzy, who looked a bit distant. I wondered if there was any reason for that, if drugs had made her sleepy, or maybe she just wasn’t interested or was preoccupied with worry about her mum.

“No, I don’t. From what I’ve seen I’ve been quite impressed with the care they’re giving to Ellie they seem very committed and Ellie is happy there.”

“Yeah,” Paul agreed, lighting another cigarette. I don't know if having a social worker speak to them was just making them nervous, but they had each only just put one cigarette out and smoked another straight away.

"Have you seen your mother?” I asked, looking at Suzy for an answer. Paul answered in her place.

“We called in there on our way,”' Paul explained, looking to Suzy for confirmation. “But we didn’t stop long.

“How did she seem to you?” I asked, still trying to get Suzy to speak.

“You say, Suze,” Paul looked round at his girlfriend, “She’s your mum.”

Suzy spoke up, her manner now fiery, as if all her repressed anger was bursting out. She spat her words out fast. “Well ... we don’t get on. Never have done. That’ll never change.”

I wondered if she realised that her mother was dying, so I questioned exactly that. “Did she say how ill she was?” I asked.

“She says she is dying. The doctors are telling her she will and to plan for the worst.” Suzy looked directly at me. There was no lack of understanding there. Though there wasn’t too much concern in Suzy’s voice either. Anger certainly, but not concern.

“The doctors told me she wouldn’t live long.” I explained with a lump in my throat. “Ellie is hoping she might be able to meet her father, and possibly even live with him I’d like to know what you think about that. She hopes to stay living on the island but she believes knowing her father would give her some comfort, since she’ll be losing her grandmother. I just wondered what you could tell us about him?”

“That’s for me to know, isn’t it?” Suzy’s tapped her index finger on the side of her nose as she spoke. “I’m not going to say. End of.” She picked up the cigarette packet and brusquely took out a cigarette, tapped it on the box and lit it. I was beginning to see, if not understand, a woman who could leave her only child in her hour of need.

I waited a while hoping the action with the cigarette would have taken the fire out of her anger and she’d tell me more. “I appreciate your point on where Ellie lives, but it would be really helpful if you could tell me something – anything, about her father. If you don’t know where he is at the moment I could help her find out, you won’t have to speak to him, I’ll do that if you prefer.”

"No. Not gonna say nuffin. It's not something I want to talk about." Suzy repeated just as sternly, her body as stiff as a steel rod.

I tried again, "it's just that if Nan does die, and doctors are sure that she will, Ellie will need a home of course. And I wondered if you had thought of taking her to live with you? Or perhaps her father? Or if you have other ideas?"

"Who said anything about Ellie moving in with us?" They looked at each other, then at me in disgust, and spoke to me indignantly. "Who is suggesting that?!"

"I did. I do need to at least check it out with you for Ellie's future," I couldn't believe what I was hearing, this woman seemed to have no compassion at all. "I know it's a sad thing to think of, but we must make plans about what will happen to Ellie when her Nan dies."

"I was hoping you'd have some ideas, about that. That's what we've come here for." Suzy answered brusquely, as if I had no right in the world to expect anything of her. At least Ellie would be spared the chance of moving in with them, I thought.

Paul looked equally offended, "What a bloody silly idea it is to ask us!"

They were both really angry. I couldn't believe that Suzy didn't think that she should have a role in her child's future, but that's dysfunctional families for you.

"Actually, it's the law that expects us to look to and ask family members first, usually the close ones. And you're her mother,

Suzy, so I have to start with you." Talk about touchy. At least I'd saved the interview, they were still talking to me. I repeated. "Is there anyone in your family or perhaps someone in her father's family that could take over her care? She is keen to get to know her dad. Could you tell me who he is and where I can find him, so I can ask if he can give Ellie a home? It's not a conversation you need to have with him if you don't want to."

As I spoke Paul and Suzy looked at me in astonishment, even as I spoke I knew I was in for a hard time as soon as I'd finished speaking.

I wasn't wrong. They were after me all guns blazing.

"You nosy bitch!" Suzy laboured each syllable to make the best impact. "Who do you think you are coming into my life and asking about things what are private! It's like I said. We think that's your job to sort out. I am not going to talk about her biological father. End of." She jabbed a finger in my direction as she spoke to emphasise the point. "C'mon, I've had enough of this! Let's go!" Suzy looked round at Paul and they both stood up to leave.

"Please don't go yet, hear me out. It's just that the innocent victim in all this is Ellie, she needs to know her options. It is worrying her. Couldn't you give me his address or phone number even? There's no need for you to speak to him, I can do that." I emphasised and looked Suzy straight in the eye, to show how important it was. But Suzy wouldn't meet my gaze.

The couple were putting on their coats. I think the only reason they showed up was to tell me to find somewhere else for Ellie. "I'll need to ask our fostering and adoption officer to look for somewhere for her then."

"Yes, you do that. You sort it out, that's your job, so get on and do it. Talk to whoever you want about it," Suzy stated, firmly pulling her jacket around her and jabbing her index finger at me at the same time, "As long as it's not me that's gonna have her. I've said all I'm gonna say now."

Sometimes talking to people feels like banging your head on a brick wall. I was telling Suzy her mum was dying and her daughter had nowhere to live, but she didn't seem to think it involved her. At least I was satisfied that I had done my best to ask, and if she was that unreasonable it was probably best that Ellie didn't go to her anyway.

Paul and Suzy made it clear that they were ready to leave, so I realised I had to go, I wasn't going to get anymore from this conversation. I stood and walked to the front door. "Ok then, I'll pop and see you again in the next few days when I've spoken to my boss about it, if that's all right. There are forms and things to fill in."

"We won't be here." Paul said pulling his jacket around him. "We've got to get back to Glasgow. We've got a gig."

"Can I ring you then?" I asked, hiding my shock that they just wanted to walk away from this situation. They walked towards the front door, I followed. I got no answer, so I tried again. "It would really help if I could have your phone number Suzy, in case I need to get in touch with you."

Silence. I stood waiting for a reply, but none came. Moments later they'd beckoned Ellie over from Greta's house and she'd ran and joined them in their car, pulling away quickly without a second glance back. They were off to the hospital.

Suzy wasn't the first mum I'd met who didn't just didn't take to being a mother, but each time it was a surprise. I suppose we all have an idea of an ideal mum, who is there all the time for you with love and comfort. But not everyone has those instincts. I never held it against them though. Life is odd, it seemed to me, there were plenty of people out there who couldn't have children and would be excellent parents, yet plenty of people biologically only too able to have children yet emotionally not up to the task.

I considered it another quirk of nature. The same with fathers. Sometimes people have the right anatomy, but not the emotional setup. All it needed was a social worker somewhere to recognise that and pair the right people up. At least Suzy was straight. And at least Ellie would never be messed about by a mum who was always in two minds, missing contact, forgetting birthdays and Christmas. We all knew these things would have to come from somewhere else.

But where else? When Nan did die, if Ellie's dad also didn't want her that could feel like more major rejection and that's assuming we were able to persuade Suzy to help us find him, there was no clue on her birth certificate. It might be better to place her in a small residential unit where they had good care and somewhere she'd know she could stay for the rest of her childhood. The last thing I'd want was any placement to break down for any reason, so wherever we put her in must be able to cope with a traumatised young woman. A placement breakdown would be tragic and could lead to Ellie struggling to trust people for the rest of her life.

I told myself that I'd worry about that when the time came. But I couldn't shake off the sense of sadness I felt for Ellie.

## CHAPTER SEVENTEEN

I was beginning to think Nan might hang onto life until I was back in Edinburgh, my time on the island had flown by, but quite quickly, things changed. The next day when I visited Ellie I discovered how her visit to the hospital with her mother had gone. I'd had a call from the hospital to say that Nan was very weak and just afterwards Ellie rung me. She was very tearful and Greta was doing her best to console her.

As soon as I walked into Greta's house Ellie snuggled into my chest and cried. I sat down on the sofa with her and kept my arm around her shoulders. "Tell me everything." I asked, stroking her hair. Greta left the room to get some tea.

"It was Nan." Ellie muttered between sobs. "Mum took me to the hospital to see her. Nan said to mum she wasn't very well, and she said to mum and Paul that they should decide somewhere else for me to live. Mum said no, we didn't need to, she didn't think Nan was as ill as she said and refused to talk about it. That made Nan and me upset because mum got cross with Nan and told her not to speak about it, but Nan said she has to so they argued."

"How awful!" I sympathised. Just when I thought things couldn't get any worse for Ellie, they did.

"Then mum said she was going back to Glasgow cos she had things to do and she'd come back the following week. So we had to leave, even after we'd only just arrived. Mum dropped me back here. Now she's just gone!"

“So she’s gone back to her place?” I asked. I was cross with Suzy, Ellie was soon to lose not only her Nan, her mum and also but me, as I’d be going back to Edinburgh soon.

“Yes. She went. She said there was nothing for her to do here and she wasn’t staying a moment longer.” Ellie wiped her eyes on her sleeve.

I got her a tissue out of the packet I always keep in my handbag. Ellie should be used to her mother by now, but sometimes she did expect more from Suzy was able to give. I guess she hoped her mom would rally round. And mum was proving that she wouldn’t.

And that must hurt Ellie.

“Shall we go to the hospital and see Nan?” I asked. Then I could find out exactly how Nan was.

“Can we?” Ellie replied with enthusiasm.

It was much later when we arrived at the hospital. We parked in the car park and walked to the ward. I could see Nan was worse as soon as I entered her room. Moved to a side room now she lay in bed, her complexion awful, there was a sort of grey and white tint to her skin. She looked as if she had no muscle tone whatsoever and just lay in a heap, hardly even holding herself upright on the pillows.

Ellie approached Nan enthusiastically. “Hi Nan.” She leaned across the bed and kissed the old lady’s cheek. At first Nan didn’t respond and I feared the worst, then, very slowly, her head turned towards Ellie, she opened her eyes and a smile lit up her face when she recognised her granddaughter.

“Hello, dear,” she said to Ellie. Nan held out her hand. Her arm was thin and fragile, skin hanging loose where her muscles had just withered away, it hardly seemed possible but it looked even thinner than when I’d last seen it. She smiled at me in recognition and welcome. I smiled back.

“How are you?” I asked, though I hardly needed to, anybody could see she was fading away.

Nan looked like she didn’t really know how to answer but then said. “Weak, dear, I’m not at all well and I can’t stay awake long. It is lovely to see you both though.” Nan said. She didn’t seem to have the strength to hug Ellie, but her words were warm and she spoke directly to her, gently squeezing her granddaughter’s hand as she spoke to her. “You are very special and you’ll always be special to me Ellie. You know that don’t you? I want you to grow up to be the best girl you can. Will you do that for me?”

Her words had a finality about them, but Ellie just accepted her Nan as she was and seemed to pick up the sombre mood. She snuggled up to her Nan, on top of the sheets, lying next to her. “I love you, Nan,” she whispered to the old lady and kissed her cheek.

I watched as the Nan fell asleep, her granddaughter snuggled right beside to her. I sensed the worst.

“She’s not talking,”’ Ellie said, disappointed.

“No, she is not well, love, but she’s still listening to you. Tell her anything you want to now.”

I wanted to make sure Ellie had every opportunity to tell Nan anything she wanted to just in case this was her last chance. Ellie spoke to her Nan freely, and told her all about her marks at school, how she was getting on with Greta, who her friends were at the moment, all about her mum, anything and everything that came to her mind. Nan responded every now and again with a nod, or word of agreement or saying "That's nice, dear," or "Oh yes," just to give the girl some recognition that she was being heard.

About twenty minutes later Nan fell asleep totally without warning, a contented smile on her face. I wondered if these were going to be her final minutes, but she kept on breathing, softly and steadily. We stayed a while longer, but eventually I said, "Nan's asleep now, we should go and let her rest."

I wanted to ask the staff if Nan was as bad as she looked but I didn't like to ask them in front of Ellie, so we left and I dropped her back at Greta's and went back to the office. I rang the hospital from there and spoke to the ward sister. I asked her how Nan was.

"She's very poorly," the nurse said in a slightly solemn voice. "The doctor's just seen her. She's going to see if there's anything else we can do, but we are concerned."

"Thank you for doing your best." I said, "If anything happens and she takes a turn for the worse could you ring me as well as her next of kin? You can ring anytime, I don't mind evenings and weekends as well." I wanted to make sure that I was around to break the news to Ellie. She was going to be very distressed if and when it did happen and Nan did died."

"That's okay. We wouldn't normally give out these details to non-relatives but we know the situation in your case you are the family social worker. I'll just make sure we've got your details." The nurse took down my phone number and we ended the call.

I wasn't surprised when I got a call the next morning to tell me that Nan had passed away during the night. They said it was probably a heart attack, they hadn't expected her cancer to get the better of her quite so soon.

I didn't want to disturb Gus who I knew would be starting morning surgery. I felt Ellie should be told straight away so decided I'd tell her alone. I spoke to Greta and asked her to stop Ellie going to school that morning and drove there straight away. I think Ellie had guessed, when I got there she was already stressed and upset. I didn't need to knock on the door, Ellie was on the doorstep, waiting for me. I had just got out of the car and locked it when she ran up to me.

"Is it Nan?" she asked, her eyes alight with concern. "Is she alright?" She was pleading with me for information yet I didn't want to tell her out in the open.

"Let's go in first, shall we?" I walked past her into the sitting room and sat down straight away. "Come here." I asked her, patting the seat space next to me on the sofa. She dutifully did as I asked and sat on the sofa next to me without saying a word, but the agony on her face was speaking volumes.

I took a deep breath before I spoke and kept my manner quiet and solemn. "You're not going to like what I have to say, but yes, you're right. I'm afraid it is. Apparently she had a heart attack in the night."

"Oh no!" Ellie shouted, her face screwing up with emotional pain, her hands covering her ears, "No, no, no! Nan can't be dead! Don't say that! She can't be!" She leant forward in floods of tears. I hugged her whilst she cried.

I waited a while in silence, putting my arm around her shoulders and hugging her to me. I let the worst of her sobs burn themselves out. Then I gave some more detail of Nan's death, explaining that whilst it was sad, it was the best possible exit for Nan, and that must be consoling if not now, in the future. "The hospital didn't think she'd go so quickly, they expected her to last a few weeks yet, but I think she knew she was going, she was virtually saying goodbye yesterday, wasn't she?" I explained calmly. "They think she had a heart attack in the night. It wouldn't have been painful they told me."

"She did know, didn't she?" Ellie muttered between sobs, wiping her tears on her sleeve. I knew there would be plenty more to come yet. I gave her a tissue. "I loved her so much and she was the only one who loved me back!"

"She loved you big time." I agreed, "I know when I saw her a few weeks ago she knew how ill she was. And she wasn't scared of dying, she just didn't want to leave you. She was very brave." I hated seeing Ellie so sad and wished I could take the pain for her but all I could do was hug her.

"I didn't want her to leave either." Ellie sobbed.

"You had a very special grandmother. Not everyone is so lucky to have someone so wonderful in their life." I hugged her tight. Sad though it may seem many children and young people don't have anyone even half as reliable and caring as Nan in their life.

Hearing the commotion Greta came in, she and guessed what had happened. She bent in front of Ellie.

"I sorry," Greta soothed, stroking her hair away from her face, "I get you drink?" she asked in her broken English and looked at me to extend the offer to me.

Much as I knew Ellie appreciated me being there, I worried about work. They would miss me if I was away too long and I had Rob to see with Gus later. I needed to be sure that Greta would be around to care for Ellie today. I hoped she could understand more English than she spoke now that Ellie had been with her quite a while. "Are you if you're around today? I don't think Ellie should go to school today."

Fortunately for me she did. "Yes, I here." Great replied, "I stay with you, we walk beach. Say prayer, light candle in church." I thought they were lovely ideas and just what Ellie needed now. I really admired Greta, she had taken in a neighbour's child in very difficult circumstances, in a language she didn't properly understand. But she was prepared to give everything, nothing was too much trouble. It was good Greta was able to look after Ellie now but what a shame she would be moving on and couldn't offer Ellie a home for the rest of her childhood.

In total I spent just over an hour with Ellie just holding her and listening to her until it felt right for me to leave her in Greta's capable hands. I knew that grief doesn't end there, it would be some months, years even, until she'd properly come to terms with the loss of Nan.

But on a more practical note I knew that I needed to get on. I didn't know who would be arranging the funeral and I guessed if there was no-one else to do it that role would fall to me. But that was the least of my worries. I knew I had to find either her father or another family for Ellie, or at least try my best. I knew how difficult this was going to be. So far I hadn't had any answers to the request I'd put out for families for Ellie and I'd have to step my search up a gear. I didn't think this would be the right time to tell her that, though I wouldn't be able to keep it from her forever.

## CHAPTER EIGHTEEN

Later that day Gus popped into me in the office when I was doing some paperwork I knew I'd need to complete before I left, and time was getting on. I'd told him by email about Nan and Ellie, - he was busy in his office and I couldn't do it in person. As usual at work my day had been busy, yet I thought often of Ellie and the situation she was in and I worried about her future.

"You'll be with me to pop out to Rob today I hope?" Gus asked standing before me in my office. "I have been seeing him at home and giving him his injections. He' is a lot better now and I'm going to stop going so often because I don't think he needs me that much anymore. But I would like your professional opinion to see whether you agree with me."

"Yes, I have it in my diary for this afternoon." I replied, looking straight up at him. I felt I could see in his eyes the bond with him I was feeling in my heart. But I had to ignore it. I couldn't bear to be hurt again.

"That's fine by me," he answered, his gaze looking at me questioningly. I knew he had worked really hard with Rob, visiting often. "My car at 2 o'clock?"

We were a team at work now, often visiting people with mental health problems together and almost always agreeing about the best way to handle things. I knew that if I only let myself relax I could be very attracted to him. But I pushed away the feelings I had of affection I had for Gus.

We were in the car when I got to tell him the detailed breakdown of the events as they were surrounding Nan's death. I couldn't help but plead with him to think of anyone who might be able to care for Ellie for the rest of her childhood.

I was delighted when he said he might know a couple who just possibly could take her and love her. But he wouldn't tell me anything about them, he said because he had to think about it some more. I didn't quite follow his train of thought, but presumably he hadn't spoken to them about it yet so I let it be. He made me promise that I would still continue to look for somewhere else for Ellie, which I agreed I would. I could hardly contain my curiosity and I hoped the new people would love Ellie as much as I did.

It was amazing how long it took to talk about every aspect of Ellie's life, from her feelings towards her father to the possible impact on her future that her current situation could have on her. It was really nice to unburden myself to someone who understood Ellie and cared about her as much as I did.

Sooner than I expected, we arrived at the stables and drove through the courtyard as we had before to Rob's home.

As we pulled up to the caravan I could hardly recognise it, it looked like a different place. The windows were shiny and bright. Each had their little net curtains as before, but this time they were brilliant white and clean. One of the windows was open to let fresh air in and the whole place looked smarter.

“Wow, this is different!” I got out of the car slamming the door behind me. I looked around impressed by the change. Gus got out and at that moment Rob opened the caravan door. He looked totally different to when I had last seen him. A smile seemed to reach from one ear to the other, he was clean and well- groomed and his clothes, still pretty hip and alternative, were neat and tidy. Pretty soon I saw why, behind him in the doorway stood a young woman, the same young woman that had looked at us closely as we drove across the stable yard on our last visit.

“Look at you!” I smiled, walking towards him. “You look like a different person!” Gus and I congratulated him.

“Meet my girlfriend. This is Natasha.” Rob smiled coyly and put his arm around her shoulders, hugging her to him. She greeted us shyly, her eyes peeping out from under long sweeping eyelashes.

“Come in and have a cuppa,” he nodded in the direction of the caravan and we followed them in. The place looked totally transformed, clean and well- cared for with a vase of flowers picked from the fields on the table in place of dirty ashtrays and old cups.

“Gosh, what a change! If the state of this place is anything to go by, you’re feeling much better.” Gus smiled unable to hide his pride in the couple. I loved that about him, he really cares about his patients. “Did one of you do this or some other fairy godmother?”

“Yeah, it was pretty much us but the support worked helped too.” Robert looked at his girlfriend, “Tash and I did most of it together. As well as you two, I've got her to thank for this." He indicated his surroundings. "I was pretty ill for a while and I didn't even know it."

Tasha bought us some tea and a plate of biscuits and sat down and joined us. She said nothing and looked very shy, not really giving us much eye contact. She seemed totally besotted with Rob, she kept looking over at him and smiling, happiness just beamed out of her.

"It's an easy thing to do, stop taking your medicine. A lot of people do that, the medicine works and people think they're better and can manage without, but before too long they get ill again." Gus explained, tucking his fingers around the mug. It was the one with Rob's name on and a cheerful message. The last time I had seen it, it was caked in dirt. It felt good that it was clean.

"You're in good company there. Nobody wants to take medicine for the rest of their lives," I said. "You're far from the first person to try life without injections, and I am sure you won't be the last." I added.

"I don't like the injections," Rob pulled a face. "But I don't like having those hallucinations either. They feel so real, and kinda take over your life.  I very nearly lost Tash," he looked over at her. She smiled coyly in reply. "I nearly lost my job, and ended up homeless too."

"It doesn't bear thinking about does it? How have they been to you at the stables to you?" I asked with concern. Not every employer or landlord is helpful when people have mental health problems.

"They've been great. I think for a while they were frustrated and didn't know what to do. But when I started getting help and got meself together like, they've been great. I think it's the island that helped too. There is a sort of magic in the place that makes even difficult situations work out alright, I reckon."

I blushed. He could have been speaking about me.

"So you're back at work then?" Gus asked.

"Yeah. They let me do just a few hours a day to start with, and now I'm building up to full time. Sometimes I come in and have a rest and then get on with things later. They don't mind that."

"How about you?" I asked Tasha. "How has it been for you?"

Her voice was much more timid and she twisted a piece of her hair in her fingers as she spoke, "I was the same. At first I couldn't handle Rob's illness, I didn't know what was going on. He kept talking about things I couldn't see and it was dead weird. But once he started to get better and I started to understand what it was like, I was okay about it."

"So you don't need us or the home care anymore?" I asked.

"No I don't think so. We did appreciate it though and am grateful for that." Rob looked at Tasha for confirmation and she nodded in agreement.

We stopped a little while longer, chatting about this and that, hoping if a similar thing should happen they wouldn't hesitate to get in contact again. But eventually it was time to leave.

"I tell you I lucked out when I came to this island." Rob took Tasha's hand and squeezed it for emphasis as they stood to wave us goodbye. "Not only did I get a great girlfriend, and a brilliant place to live, but you guys too!" The couple stood at the doorway of the caravan as they waved us goodbye.

The day of the case conference for Connor, and Clare and family dawned, and the receptionist rang me to say that they had arrived nice and early and were waiting for me. I went to collect them to take them into the meeting room and show them to their seats.

They looked like two terrified little rabbits sitting on the orange plastic chairs in the big meeting room. Clare held tightly onto her handbag, Connor slouched down in the chair, hips low, legs wide apart, arms spread out on the arm rests, chewing gum. They looked as if they were trying to be brave and tough, but I could see the fear under their masks.

I spoke to them warmly, ignoring, Connor's bold, slightly over assertive, pose. I didn't want to challenge them, I wanted them to be relaxed at the meeting. They were doing everything I wanted, and I'm sure changes were happening in that house. There was nothing to be gained by making them feel intimidated and everything to lose if they stopped working with me.

I could see Vince was sitting on the opposite side of the room, his gaze following my every move and he smiled over whenever we made eye contact. I took no notice but just nodded hello politely.

One of the senior social workers, who was Chairing the meeting came towards us looking unusually smart in a neatly pressed trousers with a shirt and sweater that toned in smartly. His long legs covered the ground between us in just two or three strides. I hadn't met him properly before but I had seen him around, he acknowledged me with his expression before approaching the clients.

"Hello. You must be Clare and Connor?" He looked from one to the other of the young people smiling and held out his hand to shake. "I'm John Woods the Chair of the meeting. I guess you're feeling a bit nervous because this is your first time, but try not to be. From what Louise has written in her report, you're doing very well."

Clare took his hand and shook it gently. Connor just ignored it, deliberately, his expression like thunder. "Yeah that's right," he said. "So why did we have to have a meeting then? We don't need no meeting, we're doing what you want, so wots the problem?" Connor frowned and glared at John. Clare blushed and nudged him in the ribs with her elbow.

"It's just our procedures I'm afraid. I agree sometimes they do seem excessive but they're designed to stop anyone falling through the net." John reassured them patiently, then he explained the procedure of the meeting, and asked if they had any questions, which they didn't.

Clare still looked tense even after John's reassuring chat, and Connor, well Connor still looked unhappy at having to attend the meeting and barely gave anyone eye contact, even when John had been and spoken to him. He sunk down even more in his chair, leaned back and spread his feet out wider, chewing his nails this time. His expression like thunder.

Other attendees joined us and sat around the room in named places. A short while later, John scanned the room, checking everyone was present and ready, before opening the meeting.

“Good afternoon everyone,” he announced. “Thank you so much for attending today, especially to Clare and Connor, who have come a long way and had to sort out childcare. Can I start by asking everyone to introduce themselves? I’m John Woods, Senior Social Worker on the island and Chair of this meeting today.”

The other meeting attendees seemed to understand how unpleasant this must feel and took pains to make the couple feel comfortable with a welcoming smile as they spoke.

"I’m Milly Peters from the admin team. I’m here to take the minutes.”

“Fay McArden, Educational Welfare Officer.”

“Vince Butler.... I work for the Child Protection unit of the police.” Vince explained that the child protection police are invited to every case conference where a child involved.

There was also Morag Jamieson, the Child Support Worker, Felicity Passmore, the Health Visitor you know, Jane Julep, the school teacher looking after Joe, and Janet MacGregor, Team Manager. Each person looked over at Connor and Clare smiling as they introduced themselves.

Clare smiled slightly as each person spoke, Connor ignored the proceedings and bit his nails constantly.

John took command once they'd finished. "Now are we all agreed we are here because of tensions in Clare and Connor's household, which have resulted in Joe being hit by his mother's partner, Connor? Or does anyone have any other concerns that we're not already aware of." John looked at each team member quizzically.

People nodded 'no' in reply. John took in their responses. Satisfied that everyone agreed that point, he carried on. "First we'll take a minute to read the report that Louise has prepared. I believe that she has already read it to the couple and you all have a copy in front of you. We'll take your comments in a minute."

Everybody turned their attention to the bundle of papers that had been presented to them and settled down to read the report. Very soon heads went up, indicating they had finished it. John began to speak again.

"So we can all agree about the background? That on several occasions Connor has hit Joe when he has struggled to get him do what he wanted? Also, to draw your attention to the medical report which is at the back. As procedures say that a child who has been hit should see a GP or specialist doctor straight away, that was done and Connor saw a doctor who agreed that the injury matched the description of the abuse and that the injury wasn't severe enough to need further medical attention or treatment. He also reported that there were no outstanding injuries or evidence of previous abuse." He scanned the room for any dissent, there was none.

People looked at each other and nodded in agreement around the table. John again scanned each face for signs of objection. But there were none.

John looked at me directly as he spoke again. "Now Louise, I understand you have been doing some work with the family. Would you tell us about that, please?"

"Of course." I spoke in a clear voice, addressing the whole group. "My work began when I visited the family recently following a request by their Health Visitor. I spent a long time with both Connor and Clare. We discussed the incident which is here in this document. Following that I asked about Connor's childhood and his approach to caring for children in detail. Connor has no experience of little children." I pointed to the place in the report that gave more detail on this, "And we felt that Connor had no planned intention of injuring Joe, he didn't set out to hurt him but he had got frustrated whilst trying to get Joe to do things. So rather than punish Connor, we felt he needed guidance on managing children and reprimanding them when necessary without resorting to violence. So we've been doing that by asking family support to go in, as well as myself, to demonstrate different ways of child management, for example how to manage baby Tom and not let him stay in his chair for too long, encouraging Joe to do as asked and so on."

“That sounds good, Louise.” John acknowledged, nodding his head at the same time. "So what is your view of the family now?"

I spoke loud and clear to the whole meeting. "There are problems at the moment, I don't think its right to try and hide from that. Connor has been looking at his own childhood to help him examine his approach to childcare. His upbringing wasn’t very good in that respect and he didn’t have good role models in child management.” I added that because it was true and might help the couple relax. “We are now looking at different ways of managing children and helping Connor develop a better bond with both children. I think with help they will be able to overcome these issues and set Joe back on track. Connor is learning well. I envisage a fairly short period of work with the family." I looked round at the couple to see their reaction to my speech, but neither of them gave much in the way of feedback. Clare just sat taking in everything in, Connor maintained his assertive posture, arms crossed tightly in front of him, jaw gritted in defiance.

"That sounds like a sound piece of work.” John acknowledged, ignoring Connor’s antipathy.

“Thank you for that.” John summarised said before moving on. “Let’s hear from the Health Visitor next.”

“Yes,” Felicity spoke confidently, “I’m really there to see the baby, who I don’t have any concerns about except that he needs more stimulation and I am working with the family on that. Otherwise I think what has been suggested is a good plan. I don’t see why it wouldn’t work because Connor seems to be genuinely sorry and understanding to me. He's learning a lot at the moment and he should be given credit for that."

Connor's shoulders relaxed a little at this point.

"Thank you Felicity. I understand Morag Jamieson has been helping with this? Perhaps we can hear from Morag next." John looked to Morag for her contribution.

"I have been to see the family twice so far." Morag explained, pulling herself upright. "I saw both parties on their own as well and we discussed the family. I took some background history and have arranged to see them again. There are quite a few things that I think would help and they were quite keen to work with me. I don't anticipate any long-term problems as long as the couple continue to work with us as well as they are at the moment."

"That is good to hear." John spoke again, thanking Morag and moving on. "Vince, do you have anything to add from the police point of view?"

"No." Vince flicked through a thin folder of papers just as he spoke. "I looked through our national database and we have nothing about either parent in any of our files so neither of them have any previous history, there's nothing more to report from us."

Connor growled, jabbed his foot against the floor and looked over at Vince, his brow crinkling up in anger. "I said that when you was at our house didn't I? You didn't need to look it up!"

"I'm sure you did." John replied in a severe tone. "But as you can imagine, we can't take a person's word for it, we have to check it out." Then John moved the meeting on. "Now, can we hear from the teacher to see how Joe has been at school?"

Jane shuffled in her chair to sit more upright now it was her turn to talk. "We've got quite a few concerns about Joe." Jane flicked the pages in her notebook, "His attendance hasn't been very good. We have asked the educational welfare officer to visit because it is so low. His achievements when he is at school are pretty poor, you can see the graph here." Jane held up her file for all to see. "But as well as that we have seen a change in Joe.  When he started at our school he lived with only his mother and he seemed to flourish. But since Connor has been on the scene, Joe seems much more depressed, his work has gone downhill and his homework isn't done so often."

"That's not right!" Clare shouted in defence. "We do work at home nearly every night and he's got better not worse!"

John intervened again, "Just a moment, Clare. You'll have your say in a minute. We need to hear whether the school have finished yet."

Clare slumped back in a huff.

School continued, "Of course we want the best for Joe," Jane said, her voice firm and resolute. "I would be pleased to see him with a bit more help in his studies. We think he needs a more settled home life to enable him to really give his best."

"Right." John summarised what he'd heard so far.

“This is a stupid waste of time,” Connor said. He frowned and uncrossed his arms using them to point at the chairman, then ending with thumping his fist on the table. “Ok, so I slipped up a couple of times. I’ve never tried to hide that and I’m quite happy to do what you ask. That should be it. End of. You don’t need to do all this crap.”

“I’m glad to hear that, Connor.” John pinned him down with a fierce gaze and stated in a matter of fact way, pinning him with a fierce gaze. “But we have an obligation to Joe to check that life for Joe changes for the better. That’s why we’re here. Do you have anything else to say?”

Connor slunk back in his seat, tutting and frowning, though still listening. “No.” Clare said.

I leaned forward to speak next. “I think Connor has potential to be a good stepfather, but he needs help to do that. I’ve proposed a Child Protection Plan that involves work from both myself, the family support unit and the school to look at managing children without resorting to smacking and to help Joe catch up on his work. So far both Connor and Clare have been keen on working through the ideas. They are early on in this stage, admittedly, but there’s no reason to think that this won’t be successful. We will of course report back at the next Child Protection Conference.”

“Thank you,” John said before turning to Clare and Connor. “The reason you’re left to last is so that you can hear what everybody has said, and then you can reply to it. Have you anything you’d like us to know or any questions to ask of anyone here?”

“Yes. You know I think this meeting is a pile of crap! I want that recorded on your notes over there or whatever you call it!” Connor stated, pointing at the minutes secretary.

“You’re quite entitled to your opinion,” explained John said in a slightly more conciliatory tone this time. “And your comments will be recorded. We’ve appreciated you working with us and joining us here. I know it’s not easy for you both.” He turned to Clare, who was still silent. “Is there anything you’d like to know, Clare? Or anything else you want to say?” he asked her directly.

Clare said nothing for a while and then spoke, “Yeah, put that school don’t know how hard it is with a new baby.”

The schoolteacher didn’t reply, but she did look over at Clare and nod in agreement.

John glanced around at each member of the meeting. “Does anyone else have anything to say?” He allowed a moment for anyone to speak, and scanned everyone’s faces, then he continued, “Now we need to vote for who agrees that the family need to have a formal child protection plan, what used to be called being put on the Child Protection Register?”

A unanimous show of hands went up. The minute secretary counted them and wrote the results down on her notepad. John nodded to his secretary, who wrote it down.

“That seems very clear, we all agree that they should be subject to a plan,” John stated. “I suggest the category as being physical abuse?” John looked around. Everyone had their hand up, John took that as agreement. “Very well, the category has been recorded as physical abuse.”

“So, wassat mean?” Connor asked.

“You all have a child protection plan, which means that we all agree that extra services will help you, and ultimately Joe at home, and you’ve agreed that is okay.” John explained patiently.

John looked around again, to give a chance for anyone to air any last minute issues.

“And now, if there are no more questions?” he looked around the room again at first, then his gaze rested straight at Connor and Clare, non-verbally asking if they wanted to ask or say anything one last time.

Connor sat with his arms crossed in front of him, a grumpy expression on his face. Clare looked from Connor to the other members of the meeting. But neither said anything.

“Since no-one has anything else to say I declare this meeting closed and we’ll meet again in two months to see what progress the family are making.”

“Phew, glad that’s finished!” I smiled over at Connor and Clare as I gathered my papers. “Now, I’ll show you to the door and will pop and see you later in the week.” I walked out with them to the door and chatted with them briefly before they left.

Vince followed me and stood behind me, waiting until the couple had gone to come up and speak to me. I thanked them again for coming to the meeting and told them I understood how difficult it must be for them. Connor’s manner didn’t change, he still looked haughty and flighty, but he was working with me and I recognised that his pride must have taken a severe dent so I remained calm, without addressing his innate anger. They stood with me a few minutes before leaving, with Connor pushing the door open aggressively out of his way.

"That was a good meeting." Vince stood in front of me, he had followed me and waited until the couple had left before speaking to me. He looked pristine in his suit, with freshly polished shoes shining out. With a file under his arm he looked every bit the smart professional.

Exactly what I am not.

"Yes, it went fine, didn't it?" I agreed feeling awkward about being with Vince.

Vince didn't reply straight away, but hugged the file in front of him and looked into the distance rocking slightly on his heels as if about to speak. But before he had a chance to open his mouth, Janet bustled up to me.

"Louise, there you are." She sounded relieved. "I need to speak to you urgently about some duty arrangements, would you come into my office now, please?"

"Yes, of course, I'll come straight away." I said. I turned to Vince and shrugged my shoulders, "Sorry, I'd better go," before following Janet up the corridor.

I'm sure I saw a hint of disappointment in his gaze. "Of course," he said, "Some other time." He walked briskly off in the direction of the door and was gone in a matter of moments.

I wasn't entirely sorry to see him go.

**CHAPTER NINTEEN**

It was the last day of the dig and just days till I left the island, and I was sad and tense about that, I had made so many friends. I didn't allow myself to dwell on it as I knew it wouldn't take much to really upset me. It felt quite fitting that the project would be ending too and I could be there on its last day. Callum had made sure all his volunteers were there to catalogue the finds and put the site back to the way it was before they started. There were a group of people replacing the soil to its original position, whilst Callum went round with his clipboard and drawings, checking they had the maximum amount of detail from every part of the site.

We worked most of the day in silence, Gus at his part of the wall, me at mine. I was very tired, it had been a stressful week and hard as I tried, I couldn't stop myself worrying about Ellie. Worry is very draining. I felt as if every scrap of energy I had ever had possessed had been totally used up. So in a way I was quite pleased when Callum said at the end of the day we should stop what we were doing and gather up any finds we had.

Gus and I stood at what Callum grandly called the finds table, although it was really just a paste table with rickety legs standing proudly in the middle of the field.

Few of the shards were big, but some were big enough to be round, showing some of the shape of the pot they once belonged to. On some of them you could see the finger marks in the clay of the person who had made them. I couldn't resist putting my fingers on top of the marks to try and connect with our ancestors.

Gus and I had a washing-up bowl and toothbrush each to clean the mud off the bits of pottery we had found. To me, they weren't just bits of pottery, but parts of people's lives and I loved the thought that people, many, many years ago, had made and used the same pot I was holding. I looked at one part of what had probably been a bowl, it had a zig zag design going around it, just like the design on Gus's jumper. I smiled at the association.

I'd told Gus I wouldn't come to the pub with them tonight, but that I was going home for a rest then would drive to my house in Edinburgh to see to my friend Cleo. She would be going back to America soon as she'd nearly finished her counselling course and I'd return to my flat and my normal life. The thought didn't excite me, although it would be nice to see Cleo.

I showed Gus a shard of pottery with some beautiful zigzag designs etched into it. He took it from me and looked at it closely, running his fingers over the design to feel its texture. He seemed to get the same pleasure from it that I did.

"I expect someone was very proud of that." Gus said as he twisted the fragment in his fingers. "It looks like it's come from quite a big pot, ye can see some traces of burn marks on the bottom. It's probably been used for cooking the family dinner."

I took the fragment back and looked at the bottom. I hadn't noticed it them before but it conjured up thoughts of family, of sitting around a fire with parents making food for everybody. “Talking of family,” I asked Gus, “Have you had a chance to speak to the person who might be able to offer a home for Ellie yet?”

I looked over at Gus, he looked strangely uncomfortable that I had asked. There was an unusual expression on his face. It wasn’t quite a frown, but his brow was definitely furrowed. Maybe it was a look of concern. He took a long time answering.

“Not as such,” He replied, keeping his gaze on his work, glancing up at me only briefly, “But I’ve given the matter quite a lot of thought.”

If I was puzzled two minutes ago, I was even more puzzled now. That reply didn’t make any sense to me. “You’re talking in riddles,” I said. “How am I going to explain that to Ellie next week? It is urgent you know.” I asked trying to hide my frustration.

“I’m sorry I can’t explain anymore. But there are good reasons why I haven’t mentioned it yet. Perhaps we could talk about it some other time?” He replied.

This was odd for Gus, he was usually so good at any sort of communication. So I asked him, “What on earth are you talking about? Ellie isn’t here, no-one else can over hear us as the others are too far away. What’s the problem?”

He ignored my challenging gaze and spoke softly. “It’s not Ellie I was thinking of. I cannae think we’re ready to discuss it with her yet, I need to discuss it in detail with them and I have nae even started, for good reasons can I add.”

I couldn't just take that as an answer, it simply didn't make sense. I turned to face him directly, I was a cross with him for being so vague on such an important issue and tried to insist he tell me. "You've had ages to think about this and ask anyone whatever you like. Anyway, what do you mean one person? You said it's a couple? Gus, this is somebody's life you know, it's not something you can leave until you get around to it. I've been trying everywhere to find someone for her with no luck. If you know somebody you need to find out as soon as possible if it's a possibility, to put Ellie's mind at rest. And mine." There was no point in hiding the fact that I did care very much about Ellie. He already knew that.

"All right then, I'll tell you." He looked up at me briefly, I could see he was embarrassed and his gaze was trying to guess my mood, but he looked down again at the muddy water and pottery inside it. "I haven't really told ye yet, because the time hasn't been right, but I am very fond of ye. Well, more than fond actually. What I was going to suggest is that we get married, live on the island, and have Ellie move in with us. We could adopt her." He looked up at me smiling, as if proud of himself.

"What!" I couldn't believe what I was hearing and just stood aghast for a moment. I furrowed my brow and thought this through, it seemed so crazy I had to make sure I was hearing right. "Hang on. Let me get this straight. Did you just suggest we get married just so we can offer Ellie a home?" He looked straight at me for a moment. I couldn't read what his eyes were saying but his words filled me with shock.

"Yes, that's almost right." He replied simply, the smile on his face vanished now. And was replaced by an expression of concern. "It's not just Ellie I want to care for, it's you too. My intentions are highly honourable, I assure you."

"I can't believe what I'm hearing," I said in astonishment. "I spend half my life sorting out problems from families that shouldn't really be together but are together because of children. How can you possibly imagine that we should do the same thing and pretend it is a good way to bring anybody up? Especially when that young person has already had a difficult start to life."

"It's actually not quite like that." This time he did look at me, he put his work down rested his two hands on the table and spoke straight to me.

I interrupted him, it was just so important. "Look, when I get married, or if I ever offer someone a home, it'll be for life. Parenting doesn't stop when the child comes of age." I looked straight up at him and shook my head with horror, "Parenting isn't something just to be started on a whim and finished when it's not convenient. Ellie's worth more than that." I got back to what I was doing. Looking back on it I was desperately tired and worried about Ellie, leaving the Island and even leaving Gus, though I would never have admitted that to myself yet.

Gus was just about to speak when Callum came up. I don't know if he'd noticed there was a disagreement between us or not, but he looked from one to the other of us, puzzled. "Everything all right?" His gaze searched our faces.

"Yeah." I replied, turning away from them. I was just too tired to think any more. It had been a long week and I still had to drive to Edinburgh to see Cleo before she went home. So I held up my head, looked from one to the other and explained, "Look guys, I hope you don't mind but I'm not gonna stop longer. I've just about done here and I could do with the time basically. I'm worn out after a busy week and I'm going away."

"I was hoping you'd come out with us tonight." Gus looked at me disappointed, "I can explain better then and I think we've got things to talk about."

"Yeah, well you thought wrong, didn't you?" I said under my breath. "Do you mind if I leave now?" I asked Callum.

"Sure. Course you can go, my love. You're free to go any time. Thank you so much for everything you've done." He answered kindly.

I put down my tools, picked up my bag and walked off down the hill, waving briefly as I went on my way. I felt used, I felt cheated, exactly as I had been with Simon. Simon had an ulterior motive, he never loved me. I just filled a space in his life. I was a convenience, an emotional stand in for when he found someone better. I couldn't believe that somebody I respected as much as Gus could have such a stupid idea. And to lead me on to think this might be a solution for vulnerable young person was just cruel.

I knew what I needed. It was time away from the island. I had got too embroiled in island life despite my good intentions, and look where it got me. There was one person who I could rely on to be the voice of common sense in this situation, Cleo, and that's where I was heading now.

Meet Cleo, my big black American friend who is staying in my flat. Cleo's currently working for Victim Support in Edinburgh to fund some extra counselling training.

I rang her straight away to ask if she was free. She was and said she was really keen to see me. I drove there as quickly as I could. I didn't get a chance to ring the doorbell, as soon as I pulled up in the car, Cleo saw me and opened the front door.

"Well, look at you!" She said, looking me up and down before hugging me tight. For the first time in what felt like ages I sighed a huge sigh of relief. I didn't realise how much tension had been bound up inside me. Cleo was like a sister, the closest thing I had to family.

She took a step back from me and looked at my clothes, all caked in mud from the dig. "You need to get straight in the bath," she said, "and give me those clothes to wash."

I was in no mood to disagree, that suggestion sounded a brilliant idea. Minutes later I was sinking my aching body into my huge old roll top bath filled with scented water.

Cleo joined me in the bathroom with a cup of hot chocolate for each of us. Thoroughly warm and clean now I put mine on the bath rest and sunk back in luxury.

Cleo sat on the bathroom chair and made herself comfortable. "Now are you gonna tell me what's troubling you? 'Cos you've got trouble written all over your face." She waved her finger from side to side as she spoke. She had a habit of doing this in a sisterly kind of way and I knew this meant she was serious. She wanted me to tell her everything and leave nothing out. No glossing over things I wasn't sure about or hiding sensitive feelings. Cleo would know if I held something back and she'd prise the information out of me. That was Cleo all over. She could read people like a book, nobody could hide anything when she was around. There was no point in telling her just the things I wanted her to know, so I told the whole story from how I'd got very close to Ellie, to Gus's stupid idea and everything else in between. I felt good for getting the whole thing off my chest and I thought I'd get a sympathetic response from Cleo.

Except I didn't.

She didn't respond straight away, but kept me waiting a few minutes while she was sitting and thinking. I could almost see the thoughts going round and round in her head like clockwork and I started to think then that perhaps I wasn't going the get the response I expected.

Finally she spoke. "You see, I don't get that." She frowned at me in a loving way. "A guy you like and get on with well makes a suggestion and you stomp off in a huff. Why would you do that? Why would anyone do that?"

"Well, he did make a stupid suggestion." I smiled weakly now, thinking surely I couldn't be wrong. Could I?

Cleo was still trying to work things out in her head. "So he says he likes you, and he wanna marry you and have this kid that you both like move in with you." The frown still hadn't lifted from her face, she looked intense, serious. "What I wanna know is why is that stupid? It sounds real sweet to me."

I laughed feebly. "Well, it's just like an arranged marriage isn't it? A marriage of convenience. I've had that before. I had that with Simon didn't I? It was easier for me to be with him because I'd been with him so long than to think about what else I was going to do. I convinced myself he was a real catch because he had the job, the money, the social contacts, that anyone would die for. Or that's what I used to think anyway. It took me a long time to admit, even to myself, that I was wrong. That sort of reason to be with someone is no good to anyone." I sensed my thinking was wrong somehow, but I didn't know why. "Anyway, who'd want to marry me?" I whispered, half to myself as an afterthought.

Cleo sat listening, taking in every word that I said before she spoke, and not just what I said, but how I said it. "Why girl, anyone would love to marry you, you is great!" She slapped her hands on her knees in a jovial, American, kind of way. "It don't sound to me like he's just talking convenience. He sounds to me like a guy that has got to know you, wants to marry you, and has thought of this little girl Ellie and made a really sensible suggestion. Why is that crazy? You'd make a great mum. I could really see you doing that."

I blushed. It was a nice thing to say. But I wasn't ready to agree yet. I lay back in the bath thinking about it. It just felt so dramatic, such a major step to take. How could I even trust my own judgement?

Cleo broke the silence. "You know what you've got don't you?"

"No. What's that?" I asked.

"Victim mentality." She stated firmly.

I was horrified, how could she say such a thing! "What me?" Surely not me? I couldn't work it out. I played with the words in my mind. It didn't make sense.

"Yeah, sure." Cleo sounded confident. "You're stuck in the blame game. You're saying it's your fault for not leaving Simon all the times you should have done. You think it' is your fault you got into that situation by being with him in the first place. You feel you can't trust your own judgement anymore 'cos you might get it wrong again!"

I thought she had read my mind in some ways. But it wasn't really my fault wasn't it? I lay back and thought. I wasn't wrong was I? Marriage is a big risk. It can't be any other way surely? Especially with a child involved.

"Listen," she spoke with gentle authority. "You was just a kid when you got together with Simon. You both could have done things differently, he could have been more like a regular kind of guy, you could have put up with it, but you didn't. You didn't want to do life his way, which is fair enough. It took you a long time to see that this relationship was going nowhere because you wanted to make sure that out was the only way you could go. And that is good 'cos it shows you don't give up on nothin' easy. But the longer you keep punishing yourself for it by stopping having any sort of love life at all, the more you prove that you're still under his spell."

"What?" I felt shocked and sat bolt upright and looked at her, frowning, demanding an explanation. "Are you saying it's my fault?" I couldn't believe my ears.

Cleo kept her cool and her sense of authority. "I am. I'm saying that ok, you got yourself by accident into a bad relationship when you was a kid and it took a while to get yourself out. That far I sympathise with you." She waved her finger in the air again and frowned like a schoolmistress to a naughty child. "But what I don't sympathise with is why you blame yourself for getting into that situation, for not getting out of it quickly, and for blaming every other nice guy you meet who takes an interest in you on the way. It's the blame game, victim mentality. You've seen it a million times before, I have too. You need to forgive yourself. Forgive him. Forgive this new guy who hasn't even done anything wrong yet. Get back to normal. Get a life. See?"

I couldn't believe what I was hearing. Victims? Blame game? I let the words float around my thoughts.

Cleo continued, her tone slightly less challenging. "You might know this theory stuff about social work, but that don't stop you feeling things in your heart. You can't just walk away from a man like Simon and not have some adjusting to do, don't matter how many social work degree's you got!"

I couldn't move or speak for shock, but I knew in my heart like a dart hits a bull's eye that what she said was true.

Cleo didn't wait for my reply, probably anxious to make sure I really understood. "What's his name, this doctor person?"

“Gus. Short for Angus.” I replied, doing what she said, but still a bit stunned.

“See, I don’t get why you say that just ‘cos one guy bin bad to you that the whole of the rest of the world of guys is gonna do the same thing. Nor do I get it that by you keeping yourself away from men for the rest of your life and staying single that is the way to perfect happiness cos that ain’t you. So one person treated you bad. Tough.” She held out her hands quizzically. “That’s life. Crap happens. But it’s got nothing to do with this Gus guy.”

Cleo said nothing more, she just wrapped her hands around her cocoa mug and waited for me to work it out.

I sat back in the bath and let the water wash over me. Her words struck me hard, but I could see her point. I wasn’t facing up to life, I was running away. Running away from myself, running away from Gus and Ellie. And maybe ruining other people’s lives in the process. I knew then I had to change.

My thoughts pondered all the options. All made sense, except one. “But how else do I stop things like this happening to me again?” I asked eventually.

“I guess you feel vulnerable, don’t you at the moment?” she said in triumph, as if this was an emotion I was allowed. “Vulnerable we can cope with. You just make sure you know about this guy well before you get involved with him. You don’t have to know him personally for years, you can short cut that. See how he is with others who’ve known him longer, see what he’s like in different situations. And look at his training, it takes years and years to be a doctor. You don't do that if you're not really committed to helping people, he ain't gonna earn that much in a local practice. What does that tell you about him? Just see where it goes. Hell, just don't blame him for the all the problems of mankind. Poor guy."

I suddenly felt very sheepish, I should have known better. "But what should I do about Gus's suggestion?"

"Go for it if you like him. I can see you like him by the glint in your eyes. You wouldn't be here asking me this if he wasn't something different to you. If you hadn't liked him you'd have just told him to sling his hook. He'd be history by now." She pointed at me. "If the good Lord is sending you a decent guy to hook up with then Praise the Lord! He must have some purpose for you!"

I smiled, she was just so loud and loveable. "If I let myself go I'm worried that I'll love much too easily?" I finally admitted and asked her, "What's to stop me making the same mistake again?"

"You is older and wiser now," she replied. "Don't you go making the opposite mistake and cutting yourself off from life just because you had one bad experience. "'Cos that ain't right for you neither."

"If I did stay with him, stay on the island, I'd have to leave my job in Edinburgh wouldn't I?" I was almost thinking aloud now. "What would I do with my house?"

"There's more than one social worker in Edinburgh. I know you is good, but you is not indispensable," Cleo explained sagely. "Anyway, they need you on the island. And you can rent your house out."

I knew finding good tenants wasn't easy. But Cleo had made me admit what I wasn't admitting even to myself. And suddenly I knew what I had to do. "I'd better get back there hadn't I?"

"I think you better had. Don't go thinking of marriage straight away, that could be too much too soon. You'd better get to know him better first. You just go and make up to him, and let God tell you what's right in his own time." Her whole body relaxed now, and a smile lit up her face. "But not right now. I tell you what I is gonna do. I is gonna get you a decent meal and a bed for the night. We'll chill out this evening indoors." She waggled a friendly finger at me. "Then you can go and head on right back out there in the morning."

"I will." I yanked the bath plug to pull it out. I felt like I had come out of the water a different person than I had gone in, as if I'd learnt something, something important, something that would change the rest of my life. Cleo held a warm towel for me while I got out of the bath. She wrapped it round me. It was warm and cosy and I snuggled right into it.

"Oh, thank you, Cleo." I fastened the towel around me and hugged her tight. This time I held her with meaning, snuggling into her ample bosom. It was the first time since my parents had died three years ago that anyone had hugged me just because they loved me. Simon wasn't very physical, but when he was he always had something else in mind. Fiercely protective, he hadn't even been happy for Cleo to hug me. I suppose he knew how close we were and worried that we'd run off together.

But now here I was and all Cleo wanted was to care for me just like a sister would do, and just as I had many years ago cared for her. I stood, my arms around her, her arms around me, for some time. I let the gentle, steady, rhythm of her heart pump against me. I could feel her care and understanding pulse into me and restore my broken heart and shattered self -confidence. It was just the boost I needed.

"You go sit," she said. "I'll bring you dinner. I got a good stew for you."

She made a lovely curry which warmed me right to my bones. I put on thick woolly socks and a cosy dressing gown over my pyjamas and we spent the night snuggled up on the sofa eating, watching old movies and drinking hot chocolate. There was peace in my heart. I hadn't felt that for years and years and it felt good.

## CHAPTER TWENTY

It was about 8.30 the next morning when my phone rang. I turned over planning to turn it off, but I saw it was Gus. My heart churned. I'd treated him so badly, so I answered it ready to apologise straight away, but our conversation didn't go as I expected.

"Hello?" I said, bracing myself to explain.

"Hi, look I'm sorry to disturb you ..." He sounded tense and worried, which wasn't like Gus.

For some reason I didn't take note of that, I was keen to get in first with my apology so I interrupted him. "Gus I'm so sorry, I've been so..." I listened closely to his voice but he wasn't listening to me.

He interrupted me now with a sense of urgency. "Just a minute! Hold on! Please listen, don't worry about that now."

"But, Gus, I need to tell you something..." I persevered, determined to say what I needed to whilst I had the courage.

"Hey, listen, its urgent!" He almost shouted down the phone, he sounded frantic, anxious. He had every reason to be tense after the way I treated him and I prepared myself for the worst, he'd probably had enough of me by now. I got the idea and kept quiet.

Once I was quiet, he spoke straight away. "I've just had a phone call from the police, and I'm really worried. I thought you'd want to know that Ellie has run- away."

"What?!" I sat bolt upright in bed clutching the phone tight to my ear.

Ignoring my shock, Gus continued. "Her carers, Pieter and Greta went into her bedroom this morning to wake her and she wasnae there. So they rang the police and the out of hours social workers. They both rang me, they couldn't get through to you."

My brain started working in overdrive, thinking of all the places she might be. Then suddenly I knew. "I bet she's gone to Glasgow, to find her mum and then her dad."

"Aye. Of course." I could hear the realisation in Gus's tone. "She'll be trying to find her mum to make her give the details of her father."

That became clear to both of us. "Ellie will be at the peak of her grief now and not acting rationally." I said thinking out loud. "But we don't know where Suzy lives. We've only got an old address."

"No, but I think I know the area," Gus reasoned, "There were just a few wee things that gave me some clues when Ellie was talking to me about her mum."

"Have you told the police?" I asked.

"Aye, but it's just a wild guess so I'm not sure they'll act on it. I'm going to take a look though."

"But you don't even know where to start!" I panicked. Somehow having one person I care for lost somewhere in the back streets of Glasgow was bad enough, having two was unthinkable.

"I can't just stay here and wait, I've got to do my bit and look." Gus continued.

Then I had a brilliant idea. "Can I come?" I was halfway out of bed, standing up ready to get dressed before he answered.

"I'd love you to." I could hear warmth and pleasure in his voice.

"You pick me up as soon as you get here," I gave him the address. "I'll find out what I can from here and let the police know, so they can do their bit."

I put the phone down and got dressed. It would take him a while to get here, and I knew it was going to seem like an eternity, but I just had to do my best and find out what I could whilst I waited.

I rang the ferry company and eventually got through to one of the staff who had been on the ship that morning. "Yes," he said, "There was a young woman answering that description on the boat early today right enough. We had a school holiday party on board and I thought she was with them, otherwise I'd have asked her for her ticket."

That was the only bit of information I found until Gus turned up. Cleo, bless her, worked wonders and gave us a cooked breakfast before we left. She insisted we eat. "You'll work that much better if you do," she said. And I knew she was right.

Gus and I jumped in his car and reached the right part of Glasgow later that day. I watched the landscape change from the warmth and safety of the car. I vaguely knew of this area, but few who have a choice find their way to this part of town. Its population is mostly made up of people from the poorest rungs of society. Many are immigrants escaping persecution, or the dispossessed in search of a better life. It was a kaleidoscope of people from all over the world squashed into a densely populated few miles or so.

"Bravender House, Queen's Road," Gus said, looking at the map on his sat nav. "That's where she used tae live, they might know where to find her now. I don't think it's far."

In any other circumstances I'd have loved the oriental smells of spice, the shops selling strange fruits, the colours of people from all over the world, often still dressed in the style of their home country. But for now I knew that Ellie would be at the peak of her grief and at high risk from anyone with unsound motives.

The sat nav gave out a few directions and then I saw it. "Over there," I said and pointed.

The road had a few houses on it, mostly blocks of flats dating from about the fifties, lining both sides. They were grey-coloured and very run down. The whole place was made of concrete in some form or other. It wasn't attractive at the best of times but in the grey murky light of an overcast day it looked very grim.

"I just hope she is with her mum." I said, trying to keep a grip on the fear inside me. "This doesn't look like the sort of area a young woman should be out on her own."

"We might not need to be here long.," Gus seemed to sense my concern. He parked the car and pulled the handbrake on.

We walked briskly to the building, and saw the flat we wanted was on the third floor. The lift was out of action so we used the stairs, taking them two at a time. We turned at the top and quickly found our number. I gave a brisk knock at the door, anxious to complete our task.

Moments later it was answered by a woman. "Can I help you?" she asked. Her eyes looked very red, her hair pulled back hard from her face. Wafts of tobacco smoke drifted towards us from the hall.

"We're looking for Suzy." I asked. "Suzy or Ellie." I asked, barely able to keep the worry from my voice.

"Oh no, dear." She crossed her arms in front of her firmly, as if she was putting up a barrier. "Suzy moved out of here a few months ago. Didn't pay the rent. She didn't give no forwarding address neither. I don't think she wanted the bailiffs after her."

"Oh no!" I gasped in horror, images of all sorts of child abusers sheltering Ellie rushed through my mind. I couldn't think where else to look.

Gus couldn't hide the fear in his voice either but he was a bit more useful than me at that moment. "We're looking for a young girl, Ellie." He turned to me. "Get that photo of her up on your phone," he asked me before turning back to the woman. "You see she's Suzy's daughter and she's run away from home and we're very worried about her."

“I know Suzy, but she hasn’t got no daughter.” The woman replied, her face screwed up her face in puzzlement.

I held the phone with the picture of Ellie on it towards the woman, ignoring the woman’s comment that Suzy didn’t have a daughter. The woman had a really good look at the screen. “No.” She looked at the screen really hard again. “No. Sorry. I’ve never seen her. Can’t help you. Sorry.” She answered shutting the door quickly.

“Thank you.” I answered. Despairing, I turned towards Gus. “Well, what now?” I asked him.

“We’ll just walk around and ask shall we?” Gus sounded rational, but the fear in his voice was still there.

“I suppose so. I can’t think of anything better to do.”

We walked around for a while asking people if they’d seen Ellie, showing them her photo. It began to get dark and we had no luck. Then I had the idea of asking in a shop. We found a place that seemed to sell everything and was open all hours. I bought some chocolate and asked the shopkeeper.

“If she’s run away she may have found her way to Dark Street.” The shopkeeper counted out the pennies into the till then pushed the drawer closed. “That’s an area which seems to attract people with nowhere else to go. Its old flats and garages near the lorry park. You can buy anything down there, knocked off designer stuff, drugs. Women. You name it, you’ll get it there.”

I felt the hairs on the back of my neck bristle with fear with every word he spoke.

“Can you tell us how to get there?” Gus asked.

“I can’t promise you she’s there. You might be wasting your time.” The shopkeeper looked straight at us, as if wanting us to be really aware of just what we were letting ourselves in for. He must have seen the desperation and determination in our eyes, because he carried on, “See that zebra crossing?”

Our gaze followed the shopkeeper’s pointing finger. “Yes.”

“You cross there and go along that alleyway between the tattoo artists and the bookies. That leads to the front of a block of flats. If you go straight ahead you’ll see the garages with the lorry park beyond. That’s the only place I can suggest.”

“Thanks.” We said and headed off in that direction. The area looked very run down it was getting dark so the area looked especially gloomy. Children played football outside. A dishevelled man sat in a porch, clothes in tatters, his teeth absent, skin and clothes engrained with dirt. “Spare a penny?” he asked us as we passed. We gave him a chocolate bar, unsure how he’d spend any cash.

The street was an area of four storey seventies flats with terraces of garages to the side. Posters announcing music nights and rough graffiti emblazoned the walls with swear words and political statements, not the elegant wall art of some towns. Old chip packets and tin cans blew around in the wind.

I huddled into Gus and slipped my hand into his as we crossed the square, he squeezed my hand in response. A football kicked by me with such force that I could feel the wind whistling around my legs. It missed me by centimetres and almost tripped me up. I wondered if it had been done on purpose and looked at my would-be assailant, a young boy aged about eight or nine, in a blue tracksuit with holes in the knees and a face grubby with ingrained dirt. I caught his gaze as the ball passed. We must have stood out in such a depressed area where people suffer from generations of poverty and low expectations.

"That young boy should be indoors," I grumbled. "It's too late for him to be out. Some parents let their youngsters play out all day and it's not good enough. It's as if they're glad to see the back of them."

"Play out all day? Play out all day?" Gus stopped and looked straight at me, delight suddenly filling his face. "You might have just solved our problem. This wee lad, if he's out playing football all day might have seen her."

I could have sung with joy as I realised how sensible this was. "Brilliant!" I pulled away from Gus and walked over to the youngster.

The boy looked surprised that we were approaching him, but he looked a plucky sort and stood waiting for us to get close to him.

"We're looking for this girl," Gus asked him, tapping the phone to bring up the picture. "Have you seen her?"

"Wots it to you, mister?" he answered, turning away and kicking his ball high in the air then catching it neatly on his knee before it fell to ground.

He stopped and looked at it once it was fully loaded, and in just a few minutes he said in a broad local accent, "Yeah missus, I seen her."

Gus and I waited for him to continue telling us where she was, but he didn't, he started dribbling the ball around his feet, ignoring us.

"Well, where is she then?" Gus asked.

"Wots it worth?" the canny young Scot asked, still kicking his ball around.

Gus reached into his pocket, for his wallet and took out five pounds. He showed it to the young lad. "Wow!" the boy said, looking straight at it. "It's real too!"

I didn't like to ask how many unreal fivers he'd seen and where they came from. The note held the boy totally absorbed, he looked at it with delight.

"It's yours if you tell us where she is," Gus prompted, half scowling, half smiling.

I'm not sure I like being outsmarted by such a young chap, but if it led to us finding Ellie, it would be worth it, I thought. At least with financial instincts like that he'll go far.

"She's away over there." He pointed towards some garages just short of the lorry park.

"What?" I screwed up my face in puzzlement. I was looking where he pointed but couldn't see anything that looked like it housed people. "But that's just for cars."

"No. Not really. People live there," he said. "Me fiver now, Sir." Gus gave him the fiver, the boy shoved it quickly in his pocket and returned to kicking his ball.

For want of any better idea we walked towards the garages not really holding out much hope of success. You would never have guessed that people rather than cars were using the dilapidated buildings, but as we watched a figure vanished into a small side door. He didn't come out again.

"We'll go and knock there," Gus suggested.

"Ok." I replied. I couldn't think of a better plan. Thoughts of murdered children ran through my mind. I struggled to stop them.

## CHAPTER TWENTY ONE

As we approached I saw a frosted glass window crisscrossed with cracks and sporting a large gap. Through the dirty glass I thought I could see a light. A very small light but a light nonetheless. I pointed it out to Gus, excited.

As we approached a woman came out of a side door. It rattled behind her on its hinges in the wind. The woman had long black shiny hair neatly plaited behind her and dressed in Indian style.

"Hi," I said and walked towards her giving her my now familiar tale and showing the picture on the phone. "Have you seen this young woman?"

She looked closely. Her gaze was scanning Gus and I as if quizzing our motives. She must have decided that we were all right. "Maybe." She replied eventually.

"Oh it's ok," Gus replied, heaving a sigh of relief. He rummaged through his pockets and pulled out his identity card. I did likewise. "We're not here to hurt her or anything, and nobody's in any trouble, but, just... well, we're worried about her. We're very fond of her."

Her gaze scanned us further, each one in detail, and then our identity cards. I stood there waiting for what seemed like an age. What if she wasn't there? What if it wasn't Ellie? What if we couldn't find her? What if this lady wouldn't tell us where Ellie was? My stomach crunched up with nerves as I tried to look as honest as I was.

“Ok.” The lady replied.

I was overjoyed!

“She sleeping.” She told us, her accent heavy.

“You mean she’s here?” Gus asked, pointing at the shabby door behind the woman. He turned back to face her, incredulous. “You cannae mean here surely?”

“Yes, she is in there asleep. I was going to get us some chips.” She looked right up at Gus and replied, pointing to the door.

“Can we see her?” I asked. I was optimistic. I liked this lady, she seemed honest and straightforward and I dared to hope Ellie was unhurt.

“Yes, go on in.” She pushed the door open for us. “I show you.”

I went in first followed by Gus. We had to file past the loo to get in, the toilet seat had vanished and it stunk. But as we passed through we came to a room which was really a garage, the floor covered with lino that was too small to fit and the gaps between it and the wall were just damp concrete. There seemed to be more garages beyond this one but I didn’t want to explore any more than I had to.

In this first garage were a few chairs in various stages of decay grouped around a wooden trolley that was covered with mugs, tea, coffee and an ancient bottle of milk. The only way to cook seemed to be a camping stove. On one of the chairs sat a man in traditional Indian dress, his sleek black hair framing an oval, kindly, face. He was lit by the only light in the room, which was from a naked bulb wired straight onto wire that draped around the ceiling and down the wall to the socket, held in place by string every so often along its length. It gave a harsh, bright light close to it but everything else was in a half shadow.

My eyes adjusted to the light slowly, but seconds later I saw the unmistakeable figure of Ellie lying on her side on a mattress, fast asleep.

"Ellie!" I called and ran towards her. She woke and turned towards me, opening her eyes just a fraction at first. I was thrilled she was safe. She smiled at me and Gus before opening her eyes fully. It was one of the best moments of my life.

"Hi," she said screwing up her eyes against the light and sitting upright. Tears rolled down her cheeks. I sat on the mattress beside her. I couldn't stop myself hugging her hard. She hugged me back and we stayed like that for a few minutes.

Gus walked up behind Ellie, rubbing her on the back. "It's good to see you're safe," he said. "How did you get here?" She wiped her tears on her sleeves. I got a tissue out of my bag and passed it to her.

She sobbed and wiped her eyes before she spoke. "I left on the morning ferry. I got talking to a woman, she was going to Glasgow so she gave me a lift." Ellie explained between sobs. "I just wanted to find my mum and make her tell me about my dad! Who else have I got!"

"Oh, Ellie!" I gasped in sympathy pushing back her hair from her forehead.

"Well it's true? Who else cares for me? My mother doesn't really want to know does she? Ok, she will speak to me, but she won't look after me will she?" Ellie looked at each of us in turn. All we could do was stay silent in confirmation. "That's why I have to make my mum tell me where my dad is."

"I see what you mean, but running away is so dangerous." I ran my fingers through her hair as a mother would. "You should have waited until either me or Angus came to see you and asked us to take you to see him or to find your dad some other way. You put your life in danger and we can't have that." I felt that just having had such a major bereavement in her life could have made her behave irrationally, so I didn't want to be too hard on her. At the same time I couldn't ignore it. In a way she'd had two recent losses, it was not only Nan but her recent recognition that her mum was never going to be a proper mum to her and Ellie knew that only too well.

"Louise is right, Ellie," Gus bent down beside us and stroked Ellie's hair as I had, "You're lucky to be safe. It's good that these people who've found you are good people."

"Safe?" Ellie looked puzzled as if her own safety had never occurred to her. Then she seemed to realise that yes, under these circumstances of course we'd worry that she wasn't safe. "Oh, Nitin and his wife Aahna have looked after me nicely."

The couple smiled at the gratitude. "We didn't know what else to do. She was just sitting down crying and looking lost. I offered her a cup of tea and she came in and talked. I thought then I could find out where she came from and help her go back."

"Yes." Ellie looked at us both to confirm her words. "They have looked after me well. They told me they've come all the way from India to help look after Nitin's aged parents."

"They don't know we live here like this. It's all we could afford. We are both looking for jobs."' Nitin looked embarrassed at their surroundings as he explained, "There isn't room for us in the main family house."

"Nitin is too proud to tell them we live like this," Aahna explained. "They think we live in a lovely house but it has lots of stairs, so we can never take them to our home. Mother can't manage stairs now."

"Oh, how awful!" I exclaimed. "I'm sure I can help you get somewhere else." I'm jolly good at finding decent flats at decent prices for people. We social workers tended to keep details of helpful landlords because they come in useful every so often.

"Thank you," Nitin whispered, holding his head up proudly.

"You must be starving,"' Gus said, digging deep into his pockets. "We've interrupted you getting your supper."

"It's ok. This is important." Aahna smiled looking more concerned about Ellie than their meal.

"If Aahna wouldn't mind coming with me to show me where the shop is, we'll get the chips together. It's my treat tonight." Gus said taking a pen and scrap of paper out of his pocket. "I'm going to write down on here what everybody wants. I want to get everyone exactly what they want, so if you're just thinking of a light snack think again and have a slap up meal. On the way I'll ring the police and Greta too, just so they know Ellie's safe."

When Aahna and Gus had gone I spoke to Nitin about housing and we swopped phone numbers and the address of his family house, so I could contact him there. At least if he couldn't sleep in the family house, it was a safe place for him to collect post and emails and I was determined to get them better housing.

We ate our fish supper afterwards with everybody and then left. I gave them some money to help with their shopping. The couple had impressed us with their honesty and integrity. There are many people who need staff like that and I was hopeful of finding them some work and better accommodation.

Later we walked across the square heading back to the car with Ellie. It was getting late and I was planning that we would go home. But I hadn't banked on Ellie's determination, nor had I quite realised how much hope she was pinning on finding her dad.

"But I can't go home until I've found my mum or dad. I haven't finished what I came here to do. I need to find my mum and make her tell me about my dad cos I have to see him and ask him if we can live together." Ellie complained, I could hear the distress in her voice. "Other people have nice dads, and I just might too."

Ellie was tormented by the possibility of having a kind father that she simply had to find. I realised she wouldn't really be able to settle in any new home until she'd resolved the issue about her own father for herself. But how to find him?

"I don't know how to help." I shrugged my shoulders and sympathised. "If I knew how to contact your mum I'd do that. But I have been trying to ring her all day, I even went round to the address we had on our file for her but she doesn't live there now."

"I can see that it's really important to you," Gus said. I felt the same despair I heard in his voice.

"Yes. Well, wouldn't you think it's important!?" Ellie stopped and we stopped beside her. "I mean they are all the family I've got now aren't they?! My mum's too busy with her music and I don't even know my dad. My mum won't even tell me about him! But with you two beside me that will make her."

"Make her? How do you work that out?" I asked.

"You two is like law aren't you?" Ellie explained.

"Mmm, a bit," I replied, wishing it were so simple. "But people still often don't do what we say."

Ellie ignored that and kept rigid determination in her expression.

"Well, she did say she'd be at Nan's soon to help sort the house out," I continued. "I expect she's just busy with her music at the moment, that's why she's so difficult to contact. Hopefully she won't always be like that. I'm sure she'll be back on the island soon." I don't know how much I believed my own words, it was probably true that Suzy was busy with music, but it was just a nicer way of saying, what is to put it bluntly, that her mum prefers her own life to her daughter.

"She never turns up when she says she is," Ellie replied with spot-on wisdom. "The only thing you can be sure of with mum is that you never know what she's going to do next."

For some reason Gus told me later he wasn't sure of, he looked to his right, and stopped instantly in his tracks. "You did say she was singing with a group at the moment did ye not?" he asked, his brow furrowed in concentration.

"Yes. Why?" Ellie looked at him puzzled.

"I've just seen a poster advertising live music. It starts in a wee while at a pub which I guess is near here," Gus stated, checking his watch. "I know I could be wildly wrong, but didn't you say she liked the music scene and used to sing with a band? I just wonder if she's with that band, or maybe she'll be in the audience. Why don't we have a look since we're here?"

"Oh yes, what a great idea!" Ellie enthused clapping her hands and jumping up and down.

We took down the name of the pub and typed the postcode into the sat nav. It wasn't too long till we found it, a large suburban brick- built pub with what looked like a steady trade in music, judging by the amount of gigs they had lined up.

Night was setting in and the pub put floodlights on. It looked like they were gearing up for the music. We got a drink in the quietest bar. The group hadn't started to play yet so there was just jukebox music to listen to. As the barman counted out the change into Gus's hand I asked him if he knew the singer Suzy and whether by any chance she was on tonight.

"Yes," he said pointing to his right. "You'll find most of the group in that bar. The roadies are just setting up, so I'm not sure if Suzy herself is here yet, they're not due on for an hour or so."

"Oh, wow!" Ellie said, "I will get to see my mum after all!"

"Yes," I said, but I wanted to urge her to be cautious, after all her mum isn't exactly reliable as Ellie has had said herself.

"Let's sit here a minute and talk about this." Gus said as we took our drinks to our seats. "I'm worried things won't work out as you want them to and I don't want you to get your hopes up too much. Sometimes things don't work out as we want them too and we have to accept that."

"No, I know." Ellie agreed, but you could see the hope was still there by the smile on her face.

"Can I make a suggestion?" Gus asked. We both turned to listen to him. "That we do this then go home? I'm not on duty till tomorrow afternoon. But it has been a long day, especially for you, Ellie." He said turning to her.

"As long as she's answered my question," agreed Ellie.

"That's a great idea, Gus," I said. "I'll text Cleo so she knows where we are too."

"Right, since we're all clear about that I suggest we go and see if we can find Suzy then."

Gus and I both looked towards Ellie for her reply. "Ok." She replied nervously. I expect she was well aware of the possible impact on her life the next few minutes would bring.

We carried our drinks round to the other bar. As soon as we pushed open the door we could clearly see Suzy, sitting on her own at the bar smoking a cigarette and watching her partner and the roadies getting the stage ready.

She turned towards us when she heard our footsteps. "Oh 'ello," she said, greeting us if not exactly warmly, then pleasantly. "What are you doing here?"

"It was me," Ellie explained. "I ran away to find you."

"Ran away from school to find me?" Suzy asked, puzzled. "What did you do a thing like that for?"

I didn't want Suzy to launch into telling off mode, what Ellie had done was very dangerous and silly, I knew that, but she was also grieving and in a very confused frame of mind at the moment and that must have clouded her judgement, so I explained my thoughts on the matter. "I think she's really feeling the loss of Nan, and just wants to know about her dad, because other than you he's her only living blood relative."

"Oh, I see." The warmth in Suzy's tone vanished completely and she turned towards the bar, away from us.

I had to keep her thoughts on our task, so I quickly backed Ellie and encouraged Suzy to be open. "I know it's probably a very difficult subject for you to talk about. I appreciate that and so does Ellie." Ellie nodded for confirmation. "But it is so important to her and would give her some comfort to know at least something about him."

Suzy said nothing for a while and I was beginning to fear the worst. She fiddled about in her handbag, took out her packet of cigarettes and lit one. Then she spoke. I was soon to learn that sometimes she looks severe on the outside when she's not on the inside.

"Sit down over there then." Suzy said. We all did exactly as we were told and all went to sit at the table she'd pointed at without comment.

She waited till we were all sitting comfortably. "Look, I know it must be difficult for you," she turned and spoke directly to Ellie. "You loved Nan very much. So did I, in my own way. I don't know what it is with me, but the motherly instinct that most people have, I just haven't got. I know I've never been a very good mum to you. It's not your fault."

"Ok," Ellie replied, listening intently.

"It was always one of the differences Nan and I had." Suzy took a deep draw of her cigarette. "She just couldn't approve of my lifestyle and I couldn't get on with hers."

"We're all different," Gus said sympathetically.

It seemed that only when Suzy was confident that she had our sympathy was she able to talk really openly. "I think this is the talk Ellie needs to have with you. I think she just wants to know about you in more ways than just a photo, what you're like, what matters to you, what sort of person you are and how she came into being. Likewise with her dad," I encouraged her.

My comment must have helped Suzy, as she carried on, "If you must know you haven't got a dad." She looked directly at Ellie, possibly to see if she was shocked or not. Ellie just sat and listened, Suzy, presumably happy with that reaction carried on. "I used to hang out in another rock band years ago. We went everywhere together. All over the country. We'd pitch out for a few days in all sorts of old cars and camper vans, even makeshift tents. We'd play a few gigs, sink a few pints, blow a bit of weed that sort of thing. It was great fun."

I wasn't keen about the references to weed and hoped we weren't in for too much detail about drugs. But I let Suzy carry on.

"That's when I met your dad. We had a fling for a while, nothing serious, just for a few weeks. Then we went our separate ways. He went back to Newcastle, where I think he'd come from, if I remember right. I was doing so much stuff, you know gear, drugs, in them days," She looked over at us to see we were still following her. We were all listening hard, so she carried on. "I never used to remember much. He was a bit rough, he had a temper on him that much I do know. I came off the worse a few times, it wasn't a happy relationship. We went our separate ways soon. I was glad when he'd gone if the truth be known. But all I ever knew about him was his nick-name was Jock and he liked heavy -metal. That's it. End of. Of course I couldn't never tell Nan that, she'd have been horrified to know that the only thing I knew about her granddaughter's father was his nick-name."

"So you don't even know where he is?" Ellie asked sadly, the truth and disappointment clear from her tone.

"No. I wouldn't even know where to find him now. I wouldn't even remember what he looked like. I never wanted Nan to know I didn't know. Nan never thought much of me anyway, I know that, even though she stuck up for me when I was wrong sometimes, but I couldn't let her know I'd let her down on that."

Suzy looked straight at me and Ellie now, as if she wanted to see what we'd made of her tale. "I have made a lot of mistakes, I know that, and she has stood by me and never said anything bad about me. But the one thing she didn't need to know is that I just simply didn't have any idea who your dad was. Not telling Nan is the one way I could hang on to any scrap of dignity.'

"So you don't know where my dad is." Ellie repeated looking very downcast and solemn.

"Nope." Suzy repeated. "Sorry to disappoint you. It isn't that I don't care about you. I do." Suzy explained. "But my life isn't a place for children, I'm just not that sort of person. Paul and I still go away with the band sometimes. The sort of places we stay wouldn't suit you. They're not what you're used to. I've always been like that and I can't see I'll change now."

"No." Ellie stated solemnly.

“It’ll always be nice to see you, but I can’t offer you a home.” She stated.

Ellie just hung her head, disappointment clear in her expression.

“I’m glad you’ve been so honest, I’m sure Ellie appreciates the truth.” Gus said, echoing my thoughts. “It is nice for her to have some contact with you anyway and I hope she can always have that.”

At least Suzy was honest with Ellie. What is really difficult is parents who offer their children a home then don’t follow through with it. We see a lot of that at work.

“I was going to look for either an adoptive family or a long term foster family for Ellie. Do you have any objections?” I asked, I and explained the difference.

“Fine. I’ll sign any papers you want,” Suzy answered, digging in her bag, finding a piece of paper, jotting a number down on it, then passing it to me. “Keep me in touch. That’s Paul’s number so use that. I’ve been staying with him so you can use that address.”

“Well.” Suzy stood up and brushed her clothes down. “It’s time I was getting ready to go on stage.”

“Can I have your phone number?” Ellie asked. “We couldn’t get through to you earlier and I’d rather have your number than Paul’s.”

Suzy didn’t reply at first, as if considering whether to part with her number or not. Eventually she spoke with a touch of warmth, “I’ve got a new phone.” Suzy got her phone out of her pocket. “Put your number in there then ring yourself, that way you have the right number all the time.”

We said our goodbyes. Suzy ruffled Ellie’s hair and went off backstage, appearing shortly after in a totally different guise, her hair brushed and around her shoulders, a long slinky dress draped around her and touching the floor.

We listened to a few numbers then went on our way. Gus and Ellie dropped me back in Edinburgh to get my car, then they went on home leaving me to make my own way from Cleo’s.

The following morning I had an appointment with Clare and Connor and I just about got there in time. I rang Greta and Pieter to check that Ellie was all right, she was asleep still so I went on my way planning to go and see Ellie once I’d finished.

I parked my car in the car park and walked up to the front door. There didn’t seem to be anyone in, I knocked harder, looked in through the front window and checked my diary. It was definitely the right day and the right time but there didn’t seem to be anybody about. I was just about to leave when I heard some people scurrying along the path behind me. I looked around, it was Clare, Connor and the boys.

“Don’t go!” Connor called and waved to make sure I realised who he was as he saw me. “We got held up.” He turned to Joe who looked right up at him. “Go and show the lady what you’ve got!”

Joe ran up to me with a fish, quite dead, on a hook attached to a line that he held very tightly. "Look at dis! I caught it." He explained, full of excitement.

The others joined me and opened the front door. All took a different task once they got in. The family looked familiar, but also different somehow, as if now they were a unit and not just a collection of individuals with each of them doing different jobs without needing to discuss who did what. I was pleased that they'd fallen into a routine now, like a team, it showed they were working together.

I took a closer look at the fish when we were in the sitting room. Joe held it up high, his face and nose still pink with the chilly air and his expression beaming with smiles.

"I think that's a little brown trout, just right for someone's tea!" I said admiringly, Joe was full of pride, he seemed free of worries and able to put his energy into things that would teach him about life. "Did you catch that all by yourself?"

"W e l l." Joe replied, stretching out the word a long way. "Nearly. He helped me!" He pointed his finger in Connor's direction. Connor had his back to us, busy with the baby.

"I only helped a little bit," Connor explained, putting the baby, who gurgled with happiness and smiled up at his father, in his special seat. "You caught him on to the hook, then I helped reel him in is about the right description. That's why we were a bit late. He took a little while to bring in."

"I see." I replied, impressed with the family activities. The house looked a lot tidier and cleaner too.

Clare bought us in tea in fresh clean cups and sat down to join us.

"So how have you all been?" I asked, looking from one happy face to another for some explanation.

"So much better," Clare enthused, obviously happy to speak up for herself now. "Doctor Gus called in, he said I was depressed and gave me some antidepressants. He also took some blood tests and found I was anaemic, so I have iron tablets now. Both have made me feel so much better but I won't need to take them indefinitely."

I could tell she did feel better, she had bright spark to her where there used to be just bleakness., Gus was very observant, you could trust him to pick up any subtle clue that something in someone's life wasn't right.

"And how about you?" I turned to Connor, keen to know how the rough young man had changed since I first met him.

"I've bin better too," he explained, sitting back on the sofa, arms and legs sprawled out as usual. "I thought about what you said like. And you was right. I got on fine with Clare but not much with Joe 'cos I never took the time to get to know him. So I do that now, and we get on fine. He's a great lad." Connor looked affectionately over at Joe.

"He taught me fishing now!" Joe called jumping with excitement. "I'm gonna be a fisherman when I grow up!"

"It takes longer to speak to kids nicely, I'll say that about it." Connor lifted his head high as he spoke with a confidence I hadn't seen before. "But it's better, you get on better with them, they get to be like a little friend and you end up seeing the world through their eyes which is great, and right laugh sometimes." The baby started crying and, without being asked, Connor walked over and picked him up. The baby smiled at his dad as he approached and I could see there was a good bond between them.

Clare sat back in her chair. She watched Connor go over and pick him up, and satisfied that all was well she turned to me. "So what happens now?"

I liked her glance at the baby and trusted her judgement. If she was happy that the baby was happy with Connor, then all was fine. I went onto explain about the next step in our procedures. "Well, as long as you keep up this excellent progress, the next time there's a child protection conference I'll be recommending that you don't need to be subject to a child protection plan any more and we can close your case."

"So that's it, that simple is it?" Connor asked, looking over to with pride to Clare and back. She returned his gaze with equal delight.

"Yes. My job was to help you see that some things needed to change in the children's lives. You did that. I can see the children are much happier now. Job done!" I couldn't help but being proud of them too, it's never easy to work with a family you also have to criticise for weaknesses in the care of their children that you also have the power to take away. The trick is to realise what a powerful job child protection social work is, and look at it from the family's point of view. Recognising the hurt to their pride that they inevitably feel and always being respectful of them was the only way to get the best out of them and help them make the changes needed to give the children better lives.

There were smiles of happiness as I left the house. I knew that this might not be the last involvement social work would have with them, they were still quite young and children can take a toll on a relationship. But they'd worked with me, they'd proved they were open to listening and would make the changes necessary. I knew there were safeguards that would be in place for their long-term futures, they would be regularly seen by doctors, health visitors, schools and the nursery who would also be diligent about watching for any problems and helping with them before they got out of hand, and I was confident that the family would work with them. I couldn't ask for more.

I drove back to Ellie's in two minds. Half of me was bursting with happiness that Gus wanted to be with me and that we could keep Ellie with us, and half of me was embarrassed about how I'd been with Gus at the last archaeology day. I didn't know whether I should apologise or just carry on as normal and let him make the first move. I went into Greta and Pieter's house with a light heart, knowing I'd need to explain myself.

As it happened I needn't have worried. Ellie was upstairs in her bedroom, Gus was with her, talking to her about the danger she had been in by her recent adventures.

The bedroom door was open so I went straight in. Ellie was sitting at the head of her bed, Gus sat on a chair legs crossed casually, to her side. It was quite appropriate for the conversation he was having with Ellie, I thought, because she'd be relaxed and she could talk openly about her thoughts and worries.

As soon as she saw me Ellie jumped up on the bed to greet me. "It's Lou!" she shouted hugging me round the neck. "It's Lou!" I sat down on the bed and she sat down too It was impossible to greet Gus first she was so happy, but I threw him a smile that I hoped said how much I cared for and loved him. I felt he gave me the same in return.

Judging by her mood, Ellie's little trip had done her good. She didn't seem in the slightest solemn or depressed, quite the opposite. I knew it would only be a temporary relief from her grief for Nan, but it showed that it had helped her to have her questions about her father resolved.

"How are you?" Gus asked, with affection.

I turned and looked directly at him., "......Gus, I'm so sorry," I said, I wanted to say more but I couldn't think what to say or how to say it. ".....I was so ...." I knew my love for him just oozed through my whole being, "..... wrong...." I dropped my head in shame. That was all I wanted to say. It was plain and simple but I couldn't explain more then. Gus said nothing but wrapped his arm around me. I snuggled up to him and rested my head on his shoulder.

It was then that Ellie gave the little speech that you read at the front of the book. I was horrified and shocked and blushed from head to foot but Gus didn't seem to worry. He just waited until I had finished thinking it through, and I turned my face to look at him, lifting my gaze from under my eyelashes.

I think he could see the sincerity and love in my eyes that burst out of me every time I saw him. I stopped trying to hold back the feelings that were bursting out of my heart for both of them. It felt so much more comfortable. What I had really been trying to do was to live a lie and that didn't work. It felt like trying to wear a size five shoe when you were really a size seven. And I hadn't been able to see it for myself, it took those around me who loved me to point it out to me.

Ellie's question was still hanging in the air unanswered. "Well, why don't you get married and then I can come and live with you?" she asked again, butting in between us.

I said nothing at first but didn't move my gaze away from Gus. He must have judged this was just the right moment. "Well, how about it?" he asked.

My heart and my mind swirled with every sort of feeling possible for a while. Should I marry anyone? Was Cleo right? What if it all went wrong? What about poor Ellie? But I knew what I wanted, I knew Cleo was right, I knew I had to listen to my heart.

"It's not something I've just thought up you know," Gus prompted me. He spoke with genuine sincerity. "I thought of it first minute I saw you, and I've been more and more certain every day since."

I took a deep breath, looked long at Gus, then at Ellie, until I finally had the courage to answer. My tummy fluttered with happiness as I spoke. "I'd love to! If you're really, really, sure you both want to be with me."

Gus walked over and kissed me, then, as if by instinct, we opened our arms to Ellie, who joined our hug. I snuggled in to Gus and Ellie this time, a position I intended to occupy for the rest of my life.

I won't give you all the details about the wedding. We didn't wait long, it wasn't fair on Ellie and we wanted to be sure Cleo could join us before she went back to the states so we had a relatively simple do. We found a lovely house big enough for all of us right near her school. It's also close to the church where Nan is buried and we pop along to her grave with either a bunch of wild flowers or a handful of seashells now and again.

Cleo gave me away since I didn't have anyone else. She went back to America with her new qualification but we'll pop out and see her soon. Suzy comes to visit sometimes, we never know when. She still isn't reliable, but it's good for her to keep in touch with Ellie. There is warmth in their relationship even if it's not the usual sort of love a mother has for a daughter. I think Ellie appreciates her visits because it proves to her that she wasn't rejected by her mother, her mother just doesn't have the sort of personality or lifestyle that is suitable for a child.

Nitin and Aahna moved to live in my house with their parents. It was empty now Cleo had gone home and they were in need of somewhere to live. I hadn't thought about it first but the good tenants I was looking for were right in front of me. They did get work in a local shop and plan to open a shop of their own soon. They've become good friends and have visited us on the island, we're both so grateful to them for what they did for Ellie and it proved what good people they are.

There's not much more to tell you now, we've settled into a happy routine. I'm expecting a baby and Ellie is delighted about the prospect of being a big sister. Our adoption went ahead quickly so we are now Ellie's legal parents. Suzy gave her consent because she knows she won't lose contact with Ellie.

It's lovely being part of a family, we all love it, Ellie, Gus and I. We spend all our free time together just doing things at home, having friends round, cooking, relaxing and enjoying ourselves. We know we'll have to part with Ellie soon, she wants to go to university to study social work. But we won't lose her forever, she'll be back with her own family in time and hopefully I'll be back with a new book and lots more adventures to tell you about.

**About the Author**

I qualifed in social work over 25 years ago in the days when social workers worked generically  and area teams visited any client group. I only stopped work due to a rare type of muscular dystrophy (more on my website) a few years ago. Now teams are highly specialised because the legal demands are so complex.

I loved the job and did every scrap of extra training I could lay my hands on, including the specialist mental health training, and the training to be a social work teacher. I studied and gained an M.A. from Bradford University in social work but I never wanted to be promoted, I just wanted to be the best social worker I could be.

I loved the job, it's both rewarding and challenging and I hope that comes over in my books.
I was always a compassionate social worker, I understood how bad it felt to have to call a social worker, and how humiliating and degrading it must feel.

That's a great attitude to have to the people you work with and I hope those I've worked with agree. If you're one of them, why not pop over to my website and say hello? It'd be nice to catch up.

Find out more about me and my work at lynnepardoe.com

**Copyright Notice**

Published as an ebook in 2015 by the author

This book does not serve as a textbook to social work practice and procedures. These have always changed regularly and it's not feasible to cover them accurately in a work of fiction. For the latest guidance in child protection procedures please see the website of your local safeguarding board. For mental health advice please see the rethink.org website where you will also find a helpline number, should you wish to speak to someone.

Printed in Great Britain
by Amazon

31307875R00155